THE
INSIDER

A Novel

CRAIG WALLER

"I have always believed that writing advertisements is the second most profitable form of writing. The first, of course, is ransom notes."

Phil Dusenberry

CHAPTER
ONE

CHRIS CROSSLEY

A successful advertising pitch must have three key ingredients: first, great ideas; second, a compelling and dynamic presentation; and third, but not necessarily last, Chris Crossley.

At least that was the opinion of the founder and CEO of the Intersect Agency, London resident and estranged son of the New Canaan, Connecticut, industrial executive Doug Crossley. *The Chris Crossley* (as the advertising column of the *London Evening Standard* had recently described him), who in recent years had leaned into his distant British heritage and been more forthcoming when he spoke about his relatively recent experiences within the hallowed grounds of Oxford, his achievement in gaining a First Class Degree and the distinction of being the first American-born captain of the Oxford University golf team.

From his Superior room at The Connaught hotel in Mayfair, Chris had peered through the curtained windows at the zinc-colored day outside and thought through the agenda for the upcoming meeting that morning. He loved The Connaught. His small coterie of friends thought he was some sort of socially fixated showboat for staying there, he was sure. But this discrete, upper-crust establishment had become a good luck charm for him ever since he had found himself in central London the night before his first major opportunity after founding the business. The marketing director at Berry Brothers & Rudd, the oldest and most famous wine merchant in London, having been impressed with Chris's ideas, energy and relentless enthusiasm, had asked him to meet his boss the next morning, and Chris had suggested an early breakfast at The Connaught as a way of impressing without fully realizing what he was biting off. The cost had been worth it, though; the agency had secured its first high-profile client, and Chris had fallen in love with the venue to the point where it had now become a new business good luck ritual. He surveyed his impeccably furnished room, with the vases of fresh flowers on the bedside tables and the polished walnut paneling framing the view to his marble bathroom, and he purred inwardly.

He was about to meet with the top brass of the Tory Party (the Tories were the Conservatives in the same way as the GOP were the Republicans, he patiently explained to his American friends). The opportunity had come through one of his former Oxford classmates, and it presented a chance to propel the Intersect London office into the limelight and put his growing advertising agency firmly on the map. Political campaigns were a two-edged sword. They were rarely an opportunity for groundbreaking work—and were, by their very nature, divisive—but they were certainly high profile; and if there was some serious money behind them, they could make or break a reputation, regardless of the outcome of the work itself. In this particular case, the whole country was preparing to vote on its future, and Chris had been offered the chance to persuade the British people to leave the European Community.

Becoming the lead agency for Brexit promised to be a potential game changer for Intersect—if he could land it.

In his hotel room, Chris rehearsed his talking points and ran quickly through the visuals of the campaign ideas on his laptop, scrolling past the research and the mock-ups of the ads. He wondered again about his choice of team for the meeting and whether the chemistry was going to work. He had recruited some of the top talent in London into his advertising agency, but he knew that a winning new business pitch was as much about the feeling in the room on the day as it was about his team's résumés and past accomplishments.

He paused in front of the full-length hallway mirror and looked semi-critically at what was reflected. It was always good to see your game face by way of a confidence boost, he thought to himself.

"A networking machine with rugged good looks and an abundance of charm. A consummate front man" was how he had been described in a recent trade press article, and he saw no reason to disagree with that assessment on this important morning. The mirror's reflection showed off those looks—the white even-toothed smile, the dark flowing hair and the creased dimples alleviated what could be described as "brooding." Instead he looked, if not cheeky, certainly attractively approachable. The long dark eyelashes had been described by a former college classmate as an "equal opportunity invitation to both sides of the aisle," and the pale gleam of the small semicircular ivory scar on the right side of his lower lip gave additional interest and a more hard-bitten flavor to the image the trade press had seized upon. There is no place in the world for an ugly pitchman, and the Conservative Party selection committee were about to get the opposite. Chris had toned down his sartorial style to a more mainstream look for today's performance: a charcoal suit, less skinny and European than most in his wardrobe, accented with a floral handkerchief cascading out of his top jacket pocket—which he had purposefully chosen in place of a tie. Completing the look was a pair of sensible, if expensive, brogues (with florally matching Paul Smith socks), all at this moment covered by his tan Burberry raincoat.

"Ready to kill it," Chris had muttered to himself as he left the hotel bedroom.

An hour later, he found himself in the overheated conference room at the Conservative Party HQ.

It was 9:10 when through the double doors of the conference room breezed the confident figure of Sir Gresham Carpenter, Chairman of the Conservative Party and convener of the contest to run the country's Brexit advertising campaign.

"Good morning, everyone!"

The voice was strong and plummy, the gestures unmistakably signaling authority. Only the weak chin and slightly rumpled attire gave away the appearance of a civil servant rather than a business titan, thought Chris as he paused to survey the room:

"Take charge" was the only thought in his mind as he stood to greet Sir Gresham.

"Very good to meet you, sir," he said, extending his hand.

Chris radiated composure and confidence, and that, in turn, as it was meant, transmitted itself to his team and the others in the room.

"Thank you for having us. Bertie said to be sure to give you his regards," Chris said.

Sir Gresham paused to shake Chris's hand, immediately recognizing the smooth power move to establish presence and leadership and to name-drop simultaneously.

OK, so this is how it's going to be, thought Gresham. This slick young man is going to need some watching.

"Bertie was generous in his praise of you and your business," said Sir Gresham. "Which is why you're here," he added. "Shall we get on with it?"

Some half an hour later and a good way into the presentation, the atmosphere was lighter, if not exactly buoyant. The scene setting and overview of the challenge had been crisply delivered by the supremely confident and unnervingly articulate Chris, who had then made way for Lars Petersen, the super smart, if slightly ponderous, lead strategist at the agency. The research was deep, the insights were penetrating, but his delivery wasn't setting the room on fire; and Emily Upchurch, Client Account Head and clock-watcher-in-chief at all the agency's significant new business pitches, was beginning to fret a little.

Lars still had five slides to get through, and Chris trusted that his impatience was being visibly transmitted through his twitching right leg under the table.

"Our poll shows that 67% of the population feels that Britain needs to be in control of its own borders," droned Lars as he pointed at the screen, which said exactly that, with a horizontal blue bar extending across the slide signaling this exact sentiment in a reassuringly Tory blue elongated oblong.

He continued, "And this pertinent (a word that Lars somehow mangled to make sound like 'pregnant') fact, plus our earlier insight that membership of Europe is seen to be the main reason why our taxes remain so high, underpins our approach to the main messaging that we shall be moving on to discuss in the next few slides . . ."

With three Lars slides still to go, Chris could feel the atmosphere in the room beginning to stultify. Always a bellwether, Emily was beginning to look like she wanted to sink into her chair.

Sir Gresham played with his cufflinks, looking at his empty notepad.

The rest of the Intersect team—Chief Creative Officer Baz Bushell, Production Director Laura James and Chief Digital Officer Swami Patel—were doing their collective best to look engaged and to keep the energy up, as they had rehearsed endlessly under Chris's direction. But data is data and Swedes are Swedes and Lars struggled manfully on.

Chris suddenly leapt to his feet. "Great job, Lars! We can see where this is going. Any questions so far?"

There was a startled jolt in the room, and everyone stared abruptly at the tall, charismatic figure of Chris Crossley, whose hitherto indeterminate mid-Atlantic accent had suddenly become very American—and loud!

"I can see what you're thinking, Sir Gresham," he said, looking at the suddenly watchful figure of the Conservative peer who'd been tasked with finding the advertising team to help take Britain out of the European Community.

"You can?" Gresham asked, with a smirk and a raised eyebrow.

"You're wondering how these observations translate into our creative approach. Am I right?"

"Well, yes, that's certainly why we got you here," said Sir Gresham, in a voice heavy with sarcasm.

"I'm assuming that everyone has presented similar research, and the rest of Lars's section drills down into why the Remainers believe Britain will be better off within the EU. We will focus a lot of our efforts in social media, particularly Facebook, where the younger demographic will be more receptive to the Leave messaging. And yes, spoiler alert, young people in our country find it hard to envisage a life where they can't take a job in Berlin or live in Barcelona while continuing to enjoy the right to be British."

"Our country?" Sir Gresham was still wearing his smirk. "I didn't quite peg you as one of us." He lightened his somewhat derisory tone with a short laugh.

Chris did not miss a beat. With his sonorous voice an octave lower, he started to speak as he moved quickly from his side of the polished table toward the center of the room: "Oh, would some power the Gifty give us, so see ourselves as others see us." Chris had both of his arms outstretched, as if preaching to a vast congregation, and the American accent had somehow morphed into a passably Scottish one.

A mystified silence descended on the room.

"So said Robert Burns." Chris remained upright and forthright, the invisible spotlight focusing on his pleasing features.

There was a pause while people around the table attempted to digest what had just been said. And why. Emily appeared to have stopped squirming.

Chris continued: "As Burns observed in his famous poem 'To a Louse," the challenge for us all is to see the world as others see it. As we know, it's very difficult to see the other person's point of view, if your own are entrenched."

Chris paused and moved his gaze slowly from face to face around the table.

When he had completed his 360, he looked directly at Sir Gresham saying, "Now, the good news is that's *our* job as an agency, and *my* role"—here Chris raised his right hand and placed it firmly on his heart and continued—"is to bring a team and a perspective to enable you to outthink and outposition the other side. And while my American accent may be seen as a sign of foreignness to some, others do see it as impartiality, and dare I say it? A strength. For it is our role to analyze the issues *very* clearly. My job is to lead a team of experts—and we *are* experts—in digital media, social media and strategy, with a deep and clear-eyed view of the challenges ahead." Then, finishing with a broad, inclusive smile, he said, "Yank or no Yank," and moved back to his chair.

The forceful interruption, with its erudite and almost musical delivery and vibrant positive tone, suddenly transformed the atmosphere and the energy in the room.

Sir Gresham had no choice but to slightly bow his head in Chris's direction and try not to look sheepish at the veiled admonition.

Chris was in full charge now, and the moment would not slip away from him.

"So, team," he said, now seated and surveying the rapt faces around the long conference table, "what do you say we assume that we have delivered our research and rationale and go straight into presenting Sir Gresham with our creative ideas and proposals? He is a busy man, and I'm sure he'd appreciate seeing how we think Britain can persuade its citizens that to leave the EU is not only a good choice, but the *only* choice for the future of Britain . . ."

The audience in the room and around the polished rosewood table were now part of the performance. Chris had begun to conduct an invisible orchestra, and everyone was subconsciously following along to the score.

Suddenly, he leapt to his feet again.

Everyone around the table looked up, startled.

Chris flung both arms theatrically above his head.

"*Let's take back control!*" he yelled. "Let's take back control."

EMILY UPCHURCH

Emily had woken early that same morning with a nerve-knotted stomach in anticipation of Intersect's pitch for the Brexit business at Conservative Party headquarters in Smith Square. Mercifully, her night had not been disturbed by her four-year-old son, Justin, although it hadn't been altogether tranquil—Brian had returned late from a darts match at the pub, and his snoring had permeated her dreams of missing trains and forgetting her laptop.

She went about doing her make-up in the bathroom as quietly as possible. Her presentation outfit of a long dark skirt, slightly risqué translucent rose-pink blouse and knee-high black suede boots were laid out on the bathroom chair from her solo fashion show the night before. Her appearance needed to be professional, but not necessarily business-like. As Chris always said: "They're hiring for the glamor as well as the smarts. We are the antidote to their boring office jobs." That had stuck with her, as had many of Chris's sayings. Hiring an ad agency allowed even the most mundane of clients access to the best thinking, the top restaurants and the most lavish parties in London.

Emily slipped quietly out of the front door of their terraced home. She was carrying a large shoulder bag that contained back-up hard copies of the presentation about to be delivered in a couple of hours. The previous day, she had meticulously prepared the personalized copies to be delivered by courier to Smith Square at 8 am this morning, but she always prepared an emergency plan. Chris had once asked about her somewhat fatalistic preoccupation with what he described as Murphy's Law, but Emily had looked back at him blankly.

"It's Sod's Law; don't mess with it," she had declared firmly, and that had been the end of that.

Emily took the main line train from Wimbledon into Waterloo station and struggled toward the back of the station to take her place in the long queue for a taxi. There her phone pinged with an incoming text message from Chris. It was, as was usual on new business pitch days, a selfie from The Connaught with a caption that read, "We've got this!"

She remembered the first time this had happened and, on that evening, when back at home, showing it to Brian.

"What an arrogant prick," Brian had commented. "Christ, what's the matter with him? He sent you a picture of himself from his hotel room?"

"It's his way of saying good luck and we're going to win...," Emily had stammered.

"Fucking hell, Em. That's not normal. What else does he send you? Is he trying to get inside your pants?"

It had been an awkward conversation with her husband. Emily knew that Chris meant nothing more than reassuring her that he was ready and that he knew she was ready. She had immediately sensed that instinctively and was both flattered and mildly thrilled by it. She knew it was harmless, and it was difficult to explain to Brian that here was a man so supremely confident in his grasp of a subject and in his own good looks, that sending a selfie was, to him, the most natural way of sharing that message.

"What can I say? He's American," she had replied to Brian. She made sure never to mention it to him again.

Once out of the taxi after the short journey across the river to Westminster, she struggled up the slick steps to the glass doors of the Conservative Party office on Smith Street. The building, like many in this area of London, looked impressive from the outside, with its stone pillars below a red brick facade with Georgian windows, but as soon as you got through the entrance, the beige carpet, standard cheap plywood reception desk and partitioned half-glassed windows behind felt like an office entrance anywhere in London—anywhere in Britain, come to that.

The impassive receptionists—one male, one female, both with black uniform jackets, shiny with overuse and redolent of the cheap nylon Emily bought only for Justin's Spiderman outfit or her own Halloween costume—sat behind a tripod with a small camera facing her. Emily had a momentary flashback to her daily commute from Sevenoaks station—way out in the Sussex suburbs—before she and Brian had moved to Wimbledon. The male receptionist looked unsettlingly similar to the train station attendant, half smug, half creepy, and she suddenly felt uneasy and not on top of a situation where she knew she needed to be in peak form.

"Name?"

"Emily Upchurch, Intersect Agency, here to see Sir Gresham Carpenter."

There was a pause, as the receptionist scanned the screen in front of him. "There's nothing in the book for him."

"Um, I think you'll find there is. Nine o'clock. The Brexit Committee. Intersect Agency. We have a presentation that's been organized for a few weeks." Emily tried to keep the note of momentary panic out of her voice.

"Oh, OK, the room's under the assistant's name. You can wait over there. She's not in yet and you're early." The receptionist's voice was accusatory.

"I was wondering if I could get access to the room to set up? The rest of my team will be here in about fifteen minutes. I just need to get everything organized ahead of time." Emily tried her plaintive, little-girl approach, in place of the authoritative boss-woman she had arrived as and who had temporarily disappeared from view.

"Can't do that until the assistant is here, I'm afraid, love. Take a seat over there. I'll let her know you're here as soon as she gets in. Thank you." The "you" of thank you rose in intonation as a final coda on the exchange.

Emily huffed quietly. Her little-girl-lost tactic had softened the response, but not changed the outcome.

She sat down on the upright chair, spreading her bags and shrugging off her raincoat in front of her. She glanced down at her phone stuffed in the top of her bag to check the time. She had hurried to the presentation venue as she had hurried to church as a child, fearful of being late, and once in transit, worried whether she had left her collection money behind. She looked around the drab reception area and took a deep breath. She closed her eyes and ran through her mental drills to detach and calm herself down. She floated away from her uneasy mental state and decided to see herself as the two uniformed, now pointedly uninterested, admins saw her—an extraordinarily good-looking, well-dressed thirty-something professional. With a bit of an attitude, frankly. She felt better.

It was time to get her shit together, she thought to herself. No point in fuming, no point in doing anything except to get her game face on and do what she always did—get all the elements of the upcoming presentation coordinated so that when the "stars" of the show arrived, everything was ready to rock and roll.

An hour later, sitting in the fetid air of the old school meeting room, Emily gazed at her boss. It was honestly miraculous to watch Chris Crossley do his thing. Emily had been fretting since she saw Sir Gresham Carpenter enter the room and register Chris's American accent with that typical British upper-class air of insouciance that came with an invisible lip curl. Obviously, Bertie, Chris's former university pal who had made the recommendation, had failed to mention that Chris was of the Connecticut Crossleys, not the Cotswold Crossleys; and Emily, no stranger to the constant riptide undercurrents of the British class system, had feared the worst in that first moment.

But here Chris was, on his feet, commanding the room and exuding the energy and charisma that had lured Emily in a heartbeat from her previous agency, had wrangled the best creative talent in the London agency scene into Intersect and had won over client after client in the past two years. She watched him work his magic on the initially dour, sulky features of Sir Gresham and marveled as he quoted Robert Burns to rouse the room and change the course of the morning.

"Always do your research, Emily," Chris had told her constantly since he had taken her under his wing.

Lord knows how he had discovered Sir Gresham Carpenter's love of the bard of Scotland, but quoting Robert Burns and not mangling the accent had been a turning point, of that there could be no doubt.

Emily knew their creative work was very strong—it was merely a question of being able to set up the moment of maximum impact to deliver it—and once again, Intersect's founder and leader had done it. Here was a man who loved advertising, loved to command a room and loved to inexorably bend people toward his will by sheer force of character as well as fluent and compelling argument. "Here is a man who loves himself," Emily could hear her husband saying if he had been present.

"Let's take back control," Emily muttered to her herself as she unwrapped the boards that showed the advertising mock-ups, fired up the video player and gestured toward the creative lead, Baz Bushell, who cleared his throat and began walking the assembled group through a series of ads, posts, videos and billboards to exhort the British public to "take back control"—a message that the agency truly believed would change the face of the country forever.

CHAPTER

TWO

LONDON—MARCH 2016

As Chris looked out of his office window, he could see the greening trees and newly planted spring flowers alongside the daffodils that were now abundant in Soho Square. It was hard to remember how concerned he had been that they were not going to win the Brexit business just a few short months ago. The triumph of the win and the raucous if relatively brief celebrations now seemed a distant memory. The effusive congratulations in the call from Sir Gresham had appeared sincere and generous, and the negotiations of the business terms of the engagement which followed were straightforward and, truth be told, very generous. Chris had assigned the "A" team to the account and apportioned a good amount of his own time to overseeing this crucial new opportunity for the agency.

If he squinted from the window north over Soho Street and toward the depressing and gaudy shop fronts of Oxford Street, he could make out the back of a billboard structure. That one was one of his favorites:

Britain isn't Working—we Want our Country back!

The tagline they had established during the pitch, and which had effectively won them the account, sat above the footer of the ad in bold Times New Roman:

Let's take back control!

He'd fought long and hard to keep "Britain isn't Working" in the mix. Yes, it was a direct lift from the famous Saatchi and Saatchi campaign from the 1980s, and that was the point. The Thatcher years had been good for Britain and its image. What some of his own team failed to realize about advertising is that the familiar almost always triumphed over the new. This was a phrase that resonated with the voters; it was a reminder of former glories—Rule Britannia, crush the Argies, all of that.

"We need the country on a war footing," he had told his nervous creative team. We're not looking for people to make a rational choice. It needs to be emotional, and Britain has always been at its finest with its back against the wall.

"We have to think of Europe as the enemy, not the beach holiday," Chris had explained to one of the young creatives on the account. The young man, Ed Vickers, a graduate from art school and dweller in a southeast London neighborhood, was clearly struggling with the idea of portraying the continent as a place to be avoided at all costs.

"Forget about your school trips to France and your stag weekends in Amsterdam; this is about bloated bureaucrats in Brussels telling us that we have to buy our beer in liters, not pints," Chris had advised Ed, who quickly assimilated the brief.

If anyone on the Intersect team was thinking how odd that a person who was running a business in Britain with an American accent and a family home in Connecticut could be speaking for the ordinary British citizen, they weren't saying it out loud. The staff at the agency were largely in awe of Chris—his energy, his accomplishments, his contacts, his confidence and his charm. He hadn't hired yes-men, but he *had* hired smart, ambitious people and was paying them well, so while there was plenty of give and take, particularly in a creative discussion, not many were going to fall on their swords to contradict the charismatic front man of the *Advertising News* Top Agency to Watch in 2016. The company had been on an upward trajectory in the notoriously competitive world of London's creative agencies in the past couple of years, and the winning of the Leave campaign had made a big splash in the capital.

Intersect had started as an idea hatched when Chris was working as a management consultant. He was there because he had accepted a job at Coopers & Lybrand just before graduating from Oxford. Following the many Brits of that generation, he'd taken a leaf from their playbook and decided to spend eighteen months traveling the world, only to return to find that Coopers & Lybrand had become PricewaterhouseCoopers, following a merger between the two accounting and consulting powerhouses. Two years into his fledgling career as a consultant in a company he hadn't intended to join, PwC sold its consulting business to IBM for $3.5 billion, and Chris found himself working for a company headquartered in Westchester County, New York, 15 miles from where he grew up in Connecticut and from where he had fled from his past to go to college in the UK.

In 2002, as he was about to leave PwC, Chris discovered that junior though he was, he had been issued a pair of golden handcuffs—if he stayed with the new owners for at least three years, he could realize enough in exercising his stock options to contemplate starting his own business. He took a deep breath, and for the next three years Chris ferociously built his contacts and a business plan to start a marketing firm. Chris Crossley and Associates was founded the week after he left IBM in 2006. With his principal qualities of great energy, enthusiasm and boundless ideas, he gradually started to build a profitable company and a reputation. He dropped his name from the front door in 2010 (as a budding adman, the temptation to riff off the word "crisscross" was too much to resist), and the result was that The Intersect Agency (to give it it's full title) emerged in 2010 as "the one to watch" in *Advertising Age*'s Annual 2007 list of top London agencies.

Chris gazed around his spacious surroundings—he had not intended to fall into the egotistical trap of the power office. When they had been scrapping away building the foundations of Intersect Agency in the variety of office venues around the capital over the previous decade, he'd made do with relatively modest personal spaces, albeit always in his own office with the ability to close the door. When they moved into Soho Square and took over the space formerly occupied by Paul McCartney's music publishing company, he found the opportunity to move into The Beatles' former office irresistible. The gift of the jukebox—a Seeburg 200, so named because it could play both sides of 100 45-rpm records—was undeniably the deal clincher for Chris, although he'd been disappointed to find that while Sir Paul had, as agreed (for a small extra consideration on the price), left the machine behind, all the discs within it had been removed. Chris had fantasized that he'd have inherited some Wings records at the very least, perhaps some Beatles and even the whole jukebox full, revealing to him (and his friends and colleagues) Paul McCartney's top 100. But sadly, it was not to be.

Nevertheless, the jukebox was a major talking point for most visitors, with its retro look, chrome finish and fluorescent lighting. Chris had arranged a selection of photographs across the wall behind, including one with Paul and George Harrison in this very office, the self-same jukebox in the background.

Now, set up on easels in that corner were some visuals for the continuation of the Brexit campaign:

"Euro Trash" a headline shouted over a picture of spilled garbage in the streets of Paris following the relatively recent strikes. The subhead—"keep your rubbish over there"—needed some finessing though, a bit more subtlety. Or maybe not, thought Chris to himself. After all, he was the one preaching the gospel of direct, unambiguous attack.

"You can call it xenophobia. I call it patriotism!" he had said in the now talked-about exchange with Home Office Minister Janella Forsythe in the recent TV round table on the BBC's *State of the Nation* series.

"Patriotism is the last refuge of the scoundrel!" she had shouted out at him, wagging her index finger.

"On the contrary," Chris had replied, in the exchange that had gone viral. "Patriotism is supporting your country all of the time and your government when it deserves it."

The silence from the Home Office minister had been deafening, and while she spluttered to recover and to accuse the Brexit campaign and Chris's advertising approach of "pandering to the basest instincts of the citizenry," the points had already been scored and, judging by Chris's email inbox the next morning, in a very decisive way. Thankfully, no one had overtly picked up that Chris's retort had been a quote from Mark Twain, which could have been a layer of Americana too far in the battle of the memorable quip that had been the feature of the TV segment.

The Brits were hard to judge on what constitutes foreignness and whom they embrace as one of their own, Chris mused. One minute he was "Johnny Foreigner," and the next he was one of them—it had been this way since he was at Oxford. I guess after a few millennia of being invaded and invading others, what constitutes being British can be in the eye of the beholder, he thought to himself. Still, he was under no illusion about the British ability to close ranks when, as they liked to say, "the chips were down." He'd seen it play out in microcosm virtually every day of his time in the country; they liked to maintain their openness and gregariousness, especially in public—which normally was a synonym for the actual pub—but the social status clues and judgments were always underlying and informing every interaction and conversation of every British, especially English, person he'd ever met.

As an American, Chris had been lucky to receive a free pass on some of the instant classifications, acceptances or dismissals by every stripe of Briton. His friends in Oxford had boasted that they could tell someone's social status within seconds of a conversation. By accent, choice of words and pronunciation primarily, but if that wasn't immediately obvious, other clues on background, education, clothing and habits would soon betray (if betrayal was to be the goal) the origins of the particular individual. Class distinctions in Britain were a complex mosaic. Regional accents were in; posh accents were out in the public sphere right now. Privilege was frowned upon, achievement and upward mobility lauded to the skies. Posh people putting on cockney accents were an everyday occurrence, especially in advertising, where "street cred" was a necessary accoutrement. But in Chris's experience—albeit as an undergraduate at the leading university in the land and then at Business School in London—the Brits were the most socially attuned creatures on the planet, and no amount of subterfuge would ever last for very long. "The truth will out" his acquaintances were fond of saying. And really, it didn't matter what was currently fashionable or not in terms of background; you were either in the elite or accepted by the elite. And in the UK, and in London in particular, this was the be all and end all of everything. Chris knew that to succeed in the narrow, visible and influential business he had chosen, he needed to pick his friends and colleagues very wisely and to play the intermediary in all ways and in all situations.

Chris knew, of course, that such hierarchies existed every-where else—he had grown up in Connecticut, for God's sake—but the Limeys took it to another level; and as an astute and attentive observer, Chris had so far been able to use that constantly accrued knowledge to his benefit, business-wise and socially.

Chris's eyes wandered over the other boards arranged and stacked for his input and approval.

The visuals were a mixture of storyboards for TV ads, bill-board mock-ups, ads and social media posts. These were both the results and the rewards of the game: the hard yards spent network-ing and cold calling; the endless hours of research and planning; the relentless repetition of rehearsals and refining the approach and then the glorious outcome of the seduction and conquest that culminated in the client win. The win was usually the cli-max for Chris—his continued involvement and shaping of the Brexit campaign was a reversion to the early days of the business when he had so few resources and people around him that he had been forced to do most things himself. That's how he had truly learned the business. In more recent times, he'd had an expensively assembled team of talented experts to hand things over to while he focused on overseeing the company and plotting the next win. Now he was hands-on again, and he was loving every moment.

Most of the ideas set out around his office were ones that they had hatched during the pitch process and in the euphoria of the winning moments after they had been awarded the campaign. Some were factual and some were emotive; all were visually strik-ing and simple to read. Chris had an aversion to long blocks of copy, and his creative team had learned not to submit those ideas, particularly in the early drafts. Hanging from the dado rail around his spacious office was a series of posters with single phrases or words in bright colors: "ADIOS" in red and yellow; "AU REVOIR" in red and blue; "AUF WIEDERSEHEN" in black and gold. He had directed the media team to buy up as many outdoor sites as they could in railway stations, ports and airports.

But some of the ideas and executions that had come through the brainstorms and passed the focus groups with flying colors were beyond Chris's cultural touchpoints and had to be explained to him.

Across from his desk hung a mock-up of large map of Europe with the British Isles unnaturally large in the top left corner that was being threatened by giant black arrows pointing menacingly toward Britain from continental Europe. The headline read, "Who do they think they're kidding . . ."

Apparently, this played strongly off a very popular TV series from the 1980s, where the opening credits showed the German army approaching Britain in the Second World War. It had been a show about the home defense of Britain. The opening titles played over an old tune whose opening line was "Who do you think you're kidding Mr. Hitler?" It was a comedy show, apparently.

Chris smiled to himself—the consequence of the UK having had only a small number of TV channels until relatively recently was that the size of the audiences was proportionately large to the overall population, and the cultural impact of hit shows was therefore enormous. He found this a lot in the UK, where people shared a common vocabulary of resonant phrases—whether from TV shows or commercials and even down to a common national curriculum at schools, where the same books and lessons formed a repetitive layer of speech and understanding across broad swathes of the population. So much so, that people often didn't need to complete a phrase or sentence when conversing with complete strangers. When Chris was in the company of Americans in Britain, they would sometimes complain about not being able to understand the locals because they "mumbled." Chris assured them that there was nothing wrong with the English diction; it was just that they each knew what the other was going to say so they spoke in half sentences and innuendo. He found it annoying and frustrating, mainly because his own superpower was subliminally understanding what triggered mass emotions and feelings— hence the appeal of the advertising industry. He hated not knowing all the clues.

Chris broke out of his reverie as the desk phone emitted a loud buzz. He pressed the intercom to speak to his assistant, Trisha.

"It's that guy who says he's from the US State Department again," she said. "Randy something," she added, stifling a snicker.

"Strange," said Chris. "Did he say what it was about?"

"He said he'd like to speak to you about an important matter. He was very American about it."

"What does that . . . never mind," said Chris. "We're an acquired taste, Trisha. Give me his number. I'll call him back."

CHAPTER
THREE

LONDON—APRIL 2016

Chris walked up from Green Park tube station toward Berkeley Square.

His appointment with Randy Gardner of the US State Department was at 11 a.m., and he was running a few minutes early. The conversation that had brought him here had been oblique, to say the least. Gardner had indicated that he had some important information for Chris "relating to his job status" that he would prefer to discuss "one-on-one," rather than over the phone. When Chris had tried to tell the guy that he had the necessary visas and work permits, and that he didn't think the State Department dealt with immigration issues, Gardner had said that it was not strictly to do with Chris's status; rather, it was slightly more complicated than that and the government would appreciate his presence for a "short meeting" at his earliest convenience. Chris couldn't help but be somewhat intrigued, if, to be honest, a little nervous. He'd had no direct dealings with any US bureaucracy since his Oxford days, and he'd renewed his work visa with the UK authorities via mail a couple of times. He ran through any possible transgressions in his head as he skirted the south side of Berkeley Square toward the address on Farm Street that he's been given for the meeting.

At the red brick converted residential building in one of those central London, tucked-away streets with a mixture of mews and three-story homes, the discrete brass plaque succinctly read "US State Department—Mayfair."

Chris pushed the buzzer alongside the sign. He walked inside the large black external door, then through another immediately afterward that clicked open as he approached it. Once inside, Chris found himself in a cramped but plush reception area, with a couple of red leather wing-backed chairs and a low table featuring an ornate eagle lamp—all situated on a deep-pile blue and red carpet. There was a small reception desk in the corner, attended by an attractive woman who looked up and smiled at him as he entered. Chris turned on his own smile as he walked toward the desk.

"Ah, Miss Moneypenny, I presume," he said, extending his hand toward her.

The receptionist looked at him without an obvious reaction.

"Mr. Crossley?"

"Yes, that's right," Chris dropped his outstretched hand by his side and maintained an undimmed smile.

"Please take a seat. Mr. Gardner will be with you shortly."

Randy Gardner came through a side door into the reception area that Chris had failed to notice, a tall unremarkable-looking man with a purposeful air. He walked toward Chris with the slight forward shoulder stoop found in the very tall. Chris saw a pleasant, guileless face and then felt an incredibly strong handshake.

"Thanks for coming in. We truly appreciate it," said Gardner. His voice was also firm, maybe with a touch of a Southern accent diluted by too much time in the UK, thought Chris. Chris was guided out of the reception area into a narrow corridor that contained a row of dark wooden doors with no indication of what was behind each of them. The patriotic carpet had given way to polished dark brown floorboards, and Gardner led the way into the only glass-paneled room at the end of the passageway.

"Water?" asked Gardner.

"No, thank you."

"I guess you're wondering why we wanted to meet with you," said Gardner as they sat down opposite each other at a plain rectangular table.

"You could say that," said Chris. "Which part of the State Department do you represent? Not that I'm that well informed about the choices," grinned Chris.

"We're interested in getting to know any US citizen who may be able to help us improve our relations with an allied country. In this case, of course, I mean the United Kingdom." Gardner, having avoided the question about the State Department, enunciated these words carefully as he looked Chris in the eye.

There was a pause.

"What does that mean exactly?" asked Chris.

"To cut to the chase—we understand that your advertising agency is handling the Brexit account for the British government."

"Then you understand wrongly," responded Chris quickly.

"Excuse me?"

"We have been hired by a group known as 'Vote Leave' to manage the campaign to persuade the people of Britain that the future of the country should be outside of the EU."

Even to his own ears, Chris sounded like a pompous ass, but he was trying to word his reply as carefully as he had heard Gardner express his.

Chris pressed on: "We're a full-service marketing and digital agency, not an ad agency. I'm not sure what our work has to do with the US State Department. Maybe you could explain?"

Randy Gardner sat back in his chair and took a breath. His hand moved up toward his face, rubbing the side of his nose. Chris noticed a small, almost imperceptible tic in the corner of Randy Gardner's right eye.

"Let's start again," Gardner said. "Your grandfather was Dick Crossley of New Haven, Connecticut, right?"

Chris was suddenly alert; this was not a turn he was expecting.

"I'm not sure what my grandad has to do with anything."

"Stay with me. Your grandfather Richard "Dick" Crossley was born in 1905. He founded and ran Crossley Enterprises until he handed over the reins of that business to your father, Doug Crossley, in 1972. Crossley Enterprises was a successful manufacturing business based mainly in the northeastern part of the country until its sale to GE in 1997. Your father remains as chairman of the group of GE businesses in which the former Crossley Enterprises sits. Correct?"

"So, you've done your homework," said Chris, cautiously this time, and suddenly aware that Randy Gardner had no notes in front of him.

"Of course. Do you know what your grandfather did during the Second World War?"

"I know he was stationed in DC as part of the war effort. My father said that he had been seconded to help oversee US manufacturing capability."

"That's true, yes. Your grandfather also played an important role in liaising with other Allied and non-aligned countries to coordinate the production of the necessary machinery for the war. He was a vital go-between at a senior civilian level as well as a key member of the intelligence department of the US Department of State. I'm not sure that you would have been aware of that."

"He died before I really got to know him. And my father has never really talked to me about what he did during the war. We all knew Grandpa as the founder of Crossley Enterprises from a business point of view."

"Of course. The reason I bring it up is to tell you that there is a strong historical relationship between the Crossley family and the State Department. Dick Crossley is a revered name within certain sections of our organization. My wish here is to explore whether we can rekindle that connection. For the good of the country."

Randy Gardner pursed his lips, put his tented and joined hands to them and looked directly into Chris's eyes, which were now fixated on Randy's tic pulsing gently and rhythmically.

"I'm not sure what you're asking me," said Chris.

"Our job here is to gather as much information on the position and thinking of the key individuals in and around the governing parties of our allies, so we can make better informed decisions on behalf of Uncle Sam," said Gardner, whose speech pattern had abruptly gone from the informal to seemingly quoting from a mission statement.

"We obviously have a very strong interest in knowing whether Britain leaves or stays within the European community. We have trade agreements, military interests, intelligence alliances and the like—all of which will be greatly affected by this decision. And as you know, the characterization of this 'special relationship' between the US and Britain has been dialed up and down over the years since, oh, I guess since we stopped being a colony in 1776. The relationship is currently a little in limbo. Mr. Cameron is regarded as a slightly elusive character. We will have a change of government ourselves this year, and our role will be to brief and advise a new President at the end of this year and going into next. It came to our attention that your agency has been appointed to manage the communications of the . . . as you rightly corrected me . . . Vote Leave organization and that organization includes prominent Conservative politicians, as well as other establishment and business figures. It would be helpful for us to have an inside track on some of the thinking and discussions that are taking place in real time."

There was a silence in the room. Chris remained impassive, his brain racing and the penny dropping.

"Are you asking me to be a spy?" he said, with a note of surprise in his voice.

"We're asking if you would consider sending us confidential briefings on a regular basis about your dealings with the Brexit campaign and the key players."

"We sign nondisclosure agreements with all our clients, and this one is particularly draconian," Chris responded. He was by now regaining his equilibrium and beginning to feel a little irritated by being so blindsided by this bureaucrat.

"We assumed so, and we wouldn't want anything to compromise your relationship with Vote Leave, and any information you chose to share with us would be 100% confidential and protected. But let me give you some more background so you're aware of what's at stake."

Randy Gardner had shifted his posture, leaning forward across the desk from Chris, picking up the large bottle of mineral water that stood between them and, making a gesture, offered to refill Chris's glass.

Chris shook his head and leaned back in his chair.

"Intelligence gathering has been a core function of statecraft for thousands of years," Gardner said. "Our job is to protect the life and liberty of our citizens, and we rely on information gathered both overtly and covertly from our friends and enemies. We also share much of that information with our major allies, and Britain is, as I'm sure you are aware, one of the 'Five Eyes' in our most important intelligence-sharing alliance. There is a 'however,' however." Here Gardner gave a wry smile

Then continuing, he said: "No independent democratic state will share *all* of its intelligence, and no government of a truly democratic country is able to predict whether it will be around every election cycle. So it falls to our small department here in this tough and gritty environment of Mayfair, central London"—this gentle irony elicited a small, compressed smile from Gardner— "to produce independent assessments of our friendly countries' political landscape as a filter through which to view other shared intelligence."

"So you're the federal BS detector," said Chris, beginning to warm toward Randy Gardner.

Randy Gardner reflexively snorted: "That's a great way of putting it, yes. If the UK leaves Europe, it changes our calculations across a broad range of issues and structures. And we have a role and a methodology that helps our government colleagues, as well as politicians, perceive and measure those risks."

"What are we talking about here?" asked Chris. "Reports, opinions, actual confidential documents that have been shared with us by our clients?"

"All of the above," said Gardner. "Much of what you share either will already be in the public domain or is being shared with us through other sources. But your unique position not only as privy to the innermost thoughts of the Vote Leave campaign principals, but also as architects yourselves of their strategy to persuade the British public to leave Europe, will be incredibly valuable to us. And as you have pointed out, and what makes this a unique situation for us, is that this is not a government initiative. It crosses party lines. It's a genuine referendum of the British people. We don't know how the campaigns will be conducted, or who is going to referee the rules, and we assess the outcome as highly unpredictable. The impact of Britain leaving Europe will be felt very keenly by the US."

Randy looked directly into the blue eyes of the handsome adman before him and said, "Unless you feel this is too risky for you? We would understand."

Chris blinked, paused again to digest the conversation and then leaned forward toward Randy, speaking slowly and clearly: "So, I'm guessing I will receive nothing in writing? And you're appealing to my patriotism and telling me that there is a family history of working with your department. And you're also asking me to break a confidentiality agreement with my now biggest and highest-profile client."

"Yes."

"Is there a fee?"

There was silence in the room as Randy steepled his fingers to consider a question for which he seemed to have been prepared.

"Alas, our budget doesn't stretch that far. But we do understand that Intersect is considering opening an office in New York," said Gardner evenly.

Another pause ensued.

"Um, it's a possibility we have been discussing, yes. We don't have the weight of presence or business to justify that yet," replied Chris, slightly less fluently. There appeared to be a frog of desire and ambition caught in Chris Crossley's throat as the words emerged.

"I'm not sure whether this might be in your wheelhouse," Gardner said, "but it appears that our colleagues in the US Department of Tourism are about to issue an RFP for a domestic marketing services agency. There has been a decision to spend a rather large amount of money marketing the United States as a tourist destination."

"I see," said Chris. "I'd heard a rumor."

"We can ensure that you are on that Request for Proposal list. You'll have to win the business on your own merits, although we may be able to exert some small influence on the outcome."

Chris was quiet for a moment. Since the agency had gained momentum after the difficult if exhilarating start-up years, he felt as if his ambition had been unleashed into an almost unstoppable torrent of energy and desire. The move into the office in Soho Square; the regular table at The Ivy; the public recognition—first in the trade press and now, frequently, in the national media—this hadn't simply fulfilled a long-held desire; it had ignited a hunger to achieve more than even he had known was there. An office on Madison Avenue was at the top of his list of next steps in the evolution of Intersect.

Chris's thoughts rushed to the escape from Connecticut that had brought him to the UK following the falling out with his family. He remembered the privileged childhood he had left behind and the early difficulties he had assimilating at Oxford. He recalled the hard graft of his professional career and the long days and nights of establishing his business alone. He had always yearned for success and thought, until this meeting, that his ambition was limited to his adopted country for now.

But listening to Randy Gardner, he realized how much there was still left in front of him. The US government needed his help to formulate its plans at a geopolitical level. By becoming a spy, he could accelerate the growth of his business in the US with very little risk. And despite himself, he found that prospect rather thrilling. He had left his office that morning for an unknown meeting with an obscure branch of the US State Department with very little expectation. In the course of an hour, he had discovered that his grandfather was a revered patriot and that he could join an honorable family tradition by helping his country. Of course, he *must* grasp the opportunity to open an office on Madison Avenue! Chris Crossley, CEO of Intersect, had the opportunity to become a figure of transatlantic importance. He made his decision.

"How is this going to work, exactly?"

CHAPTER
FOUR

LONDON—MAY 2016

Chris had long been a walker through the streets of London. Once he had figured out the geography of the city when he came down from Oxford, he realized that it was sometimes the fastest and always the easiest way to get around. London was a walking city, and he relished finding shortcuts and alleyways that had been explored and used for hundreds of years. As he left the anonymous entrance of the State Department office, he cut across Berkeley Square, past the Rolls Royce dealership—he'd always wondered whether Charles Barclay (the name proudly emblazoned over the gleaming car showroom) had chosen the venue of his car company solely for the name. From there he wandered past the designer storefronts of New Bond Street, moved carefully across Regent Street, skirted the grubby and touristy Carnaby Street and made his merry way into Soho. He'd texted his newly promoted and now grandly titled Head of Client Services, Emily Upchurch, to meet him at the Dog & Duck pub just off Frith Street. It was scarcely 12:30, but he needed to think, drink and talk things through.

Emily had been an early hire and a relatively junior account manager when he had started Intersect five years earlier, and she had flourished ever since, gathering the confidence of the clients, her colleagues and particularly Chris. He had to admit that when he first hired her, he was unsure of her full potential. At the time he needed an inexpensive, well-trained account manager from a big London agency to help add some credibility to the start-up. The fact that she was all those things and incredibly attractive fitted Chris's need for Intersect to be the "cool kids in town." He had traded on his own looks and was an avid subscriber to the "pretty privilege" theory. As well as being beautiful, she was both smart and discrete—qualities he prized highly.

The Dog & Duck was already busy, and he found Emily fiercely defending a tiny table with two stools next to the back wall of the downstairs bar, known for its Victorian tilework and being constantly full of drinkers—both local and tourist.

"Thanks, Em," he said.

"No problem. I got you a Peroni—hope that's OK?"

"Sure, cheers. What's going on?"

"You tell me—is there a problem I need to know about?"

"What would make you think that?" said Chris with a grin.

"Oh, I don't know. The text message to meet you outside the office; a pub, not a restaurant. ASAP. It's feeling a little mysterious."

"How's it going with the Leave campaign?"

Chris was obviously going to keep her waiting, thought Emily. "It's going well, I think. We just wrapped the 30-second spot and are moving onto the digital buys. Although Sir Gresham is still more involved than we'd like. You should have lunch with him; he's still grumbling about the 'Britain isn't Working' executions. I'm sure you can calm him down."

"OK, will do. Can you set a meeting to review the new stuff this afternoon? I'm not seeing these ideas until they're almost fully baked, and then it's twice as hard to make changes."

Emily paused—the constant refereeing between the creative department and her boss was wearing her down; each side was a strong advocate of its views, and it felt more and more like each was trying to use her as a proxy in an increasingly personal fight.

"While you're making lunch appointments, what about inviting Baz?" she ventured, referring to Intersect's Chief Creative Officer, Baz Bushell. "The vibe isn't great at the moment, and you two should get together outside of the office once in a while."

Emily winced inwardly as those words escaped. Chris was very touchy when it came to overstepping, and she never knew exactly when those boundaries would be breached. At the same time, she knew that Chris relied on her for an accurate reading of the constantly fluctuating moods in the creative agency.

Instead of answering, Chris gazed across the pub, his eyes seemingly glazed over as the bright sunlight filtered in, sending flashes of reflective light around the now busy, noisy bar. The light sparkled off the regimented platoons of different-sized and -colored liquor bottles, glinted off the metallic-edged beer taps and shimmered from the brightly glazed green and earth wall tiles. The hum of conversation cocooned them.

"Do you think we're doing the right thing, Em?" he asked quietly.

She strained a little to hear him and leaned forward. "How do you mean? Creatively?"

"No, I mean did we pick the right side? Are we doing the right thing? Is Brexit the right choice for the country?"

"Is this a test?" Emily said, startled.

Chris shook his head. "No, not at all. There's just so much rancor. It's feeling a bit unnerving. We're a marketing agency, and we seem to be playing a ridiculously outsized role in determining the future of this country—which, don't get me wrong, I don't mind for our visibility. They asked for an appeal to the gut, and we're giving it to them. Don't you get the feeling that we're being set up by the pols as a scapegoat, in case it gets too nasty? And now we're being accused of setting neighbor against neighbor. It doesn't bother me too much, but I see it and I guess I'm asking you how you feel about it."

Emily paused. This was a very un–Chris Crossley moment, she thought to herself. Those piercing blue eyes under the almost mascaraed dark lashes were fixed on her.

"Um, I supposed we were treating it like a normal client assignment. We were awarded the business after a competitive pitch and were given a brief, and now we're trying to fulfill that to the best of our ability. It's going to make the agency famous. And make us money." Emily realized her job here was to tell Chris what he wanted to hear.

"Yes, all that is true," said Chris. "I guess all I'm thinking is that if had been a pharma business or, God forbid, a tobacco business, or even a liquor account, we'd have had the ethics conversation."

"Yeah, you kind of railroaded us through that," said Emily.

"How do you mean?"

"The speech about we're on the side of democracy—a referendum is a national debate, and we're merely articulating one point of view."

"I guess I said that," muttered Chris.

"What's the problem?" asked Emily again.

"Oh, I don't know. I guess it's the vitriol, the graffiti, the gravity of it all. And all the infighting—who'd have thought all these 'Leave' factions would emerge? They are all meant to be on the same side, but now we've got splinter Leave groups running around like headless chickens. And that fool, Farage. I know winning the account was everything we wanted. I'm looking for some reassurance I suppose."

"We are the tip of the spear, to use another Crossley-ism," smiled Emily. "It's meant to be uncomfortable."

Chris laughed. "My round."

By the time Chris returned with another pint and a Chardonnay, the space around the table was even more crowded. Chris sat down on the small stool, his knee jammed against Emily's thigh.

"Sorry about that," he said.

Emily was also awkwardly seated on a matching low stool. She looked across at him—her low-cut blue dress just revealing a black lace bra, her smile, Chris suddenly thought to himself, could be construed as seductive.

"No worries, Mr. Crossley."

She had good teeth, thought Chris. Gorgeous eyes too, now to think about it. He'd always been aware of her great body—she, like him, had been a college athlete, something they had bonded over during her first job interview.

"Cheers!" he said. "You're the best, Em. You look great!"

There was a jolt of electricity between the two of them. They were both immediately aware of it. Chris felt a stirring, as unexpected as it was strong. He kept his knee against Emily's thigh for a moment and increased the pressure slightly. Then they both pulled apart, guiltily, and carried on the conversation, aware, if disconcerted.

"So, what do you need from me?" asked Emily, flushing slightly and aware of a loud, if unintended, double entendre in her ears.

Chris ran his tongue around his lips as he finished a swallow from his pint glass.

Emily tried not to be obviously staring. The noise in the room seemed to recede.

"Reports!" said Chris abruptly, breaking the spell. "Could you send me every contact report with Vote Leave since we started?"

"I'm sure you've been cc'd on them all," said Emily, aware that the moment, whatever moment it had been, was over.

"Not the summaries," said Chris. "The full transcripts of the meetings. All the Gove and Boris Johnson conversations and comments. We may need them at a future date. I want to be sure they are captured. Every detail is important. They may very well be part of history."

"Sure," said Emily. "I'll bundle them all into one document and send it to you."

"And a hard copy too," said Chris.

Emily looked at him quizzically. "That's a lot of paper. Are you sure?"

"I just want to be sure we have hard copies."

"I can print them off and keep them safe if you want."

"No, that's OK. I'll keep ahold of them," said Chris. "Chain of custody and all that."

Emily knew when she had received an order and kept her counsel. It seemed very odd to her. Chris had always asked for his inbox to be kept to the bare minimum, and he'd never asked for back-up before. He must be truly freaked out about this, she thought.

Mind you, she was happy to hear him ask about morale. She had to admit that the campaign was beginning to affect everyone in the agency. Her mother had taken her to task over the phone on the weekend, to put it mildly.

"Why are you helping those lying idiots?" had been her exact words.

She had spent time talking to her mother about the work that Intersect had been doing, explaining that it was to support a point of view and a position. It was a debate for the whole country to judge, and people need to be in possession of the facts she had said, quoting Chris practically verbatim.

Her mother's responses were polite but distant. She and Emily's father had a timeshare in Malaga and were taking the whole Brexit thing very personally. They had spent their lives saving for a "place abroad" and looked forward to their fortnight in late spring and their week in September as the highlight of their year. No amount of reassurance that they would be able to continue their idyllic lifestyle post-Brexit made an impression. "Fucking Tory snobs, what do they know?" was her father's refrain—it had been his motto for most of Emily's life, a fact that had made her very self-conscious growing up in Sevenoaks.

The upcoming Brexit vote had made her father even more vitriolic, if that was possible. No amount of pointing out that Brexit was not exclusively tied to any one political party made any headway with him. "Look at that wanker, Boris Johnson," he would fume on the floral sofa in front of the television evening news. "What does he know about anything? Silver spoon, public school wanker." "Wanker" was her father's favorite word—and Emily, having now attended four "Vote Leave" meetings with the Lord Mayor of London, Alexander Boris de Pfeffel Johnson, in attendance, was not in complete disagreement with her father's assessment.

"So, good to go?" asked Chris. "Thanks for the drink, Emily. Don't forget to put it on your expenses." He extended his hand for her as she raised herself from the low stool. His hand felt strong and cool and emitted the same electric current as the thigh/knee collaboration moments earlier. They walked out of the Dog & Duck and crossed Frith Street to head back toward the office.

Chris put his hand on Emily's shoulder, and she turned to look at him:

"How would your husband feel about you spending some time in New York?" he asked.

CHAPTER

FIVE

DALLAS—MAY 2016

Connie Ross Butterworth, tall—some would say statuesque—and as sleek as the *Cutty Sark* and elegantly dressed in a mid-length skirt, bronze blouse, white jacket, pearls and sensible mid-heel shoes, walked across the parking lot of Al Biernat's, having parked her BMW in the parking lot of the tony Highland Park restaurant. The sound of grackles squawking at each other from the hackberry trees that surrounded the lot was startlingly loud and made Connie think of the long hot Texas summer that was ahead.

The black hairband holding her cascading red hair in place was studded with small precious stones that sparkled in the warm sunlight of the bright May day. Connie breezed through the entranceway and up to the desk.

"Dennis, how are you?" It was less of a question and more of a statement, delivered with an emphatic, Southern-tinged bark.

"Mrs. Butterworth, how wonderful to see you. Your table is waiting." The maître d moved swiftly from behind the upright lectern, swooping up a menu.

"Your guest is here," he told her.

"Perfect!" Connie strode across the dining area, head high, her long white, almost alabaster neck craning forward and sideways, giraffe-like, to survey the room as she crossed it purposefully. Here she nodded; there she smiled; just once she raised her hand to waist level to acknowledge a seated diner of her acquaintance.

She paused at the window table for two as her guest rose to his feet to extend his hand. This she ignored and leaned her face toward his, offering her cheek. The pale neck quivered, and the subterranean cobalt veins therein seemed to visibly throb as Walt Meyer, partner in the venerable Dallas law firm, Meyer & Meyer, leaned forward to brush his lips against Connie's proffered left cheek.

"Walter, how good to see you!" exclaimed Connie loudly, to address the audience of diners as much as to greet her guest.

She stood aside, while Dennis, the maître d, pulled out her chair and Walt, hitherto rarely Walter, waited for his client to be seated.

Meyer & Meyer had represented the Butterworth business for decades, as long as anyone in either firm could remember. Old man Butterworth and Walter Meyer Sr. had schemed their way through north Texas commercial life and society for decades, doing deals that enabled the Butterworth business to move from a downtown haberdashery to the ultimate high-end department store that defined the Dallas social scene, establishing spin-offs and subsidiaries—from interior design to confectionery—that had made the Butterworth name synonymous with style, fashion and success. And if there was one quality prized above all others in the Dallas/Fort Worth area, it was success.

When the department store developed its customer catalog and then grew that division into a stand-alone unit, it had become Connie's practical MBA in place of having to actually go to college. Butterworth Catalogs had grown from an in-house department of a dozen people to a national powerhouse under her beady-eyed watch, producing catalogs for retailers, tech companies, business-to-business suppliers and direct-to-consumer manufacturers, not only in Texas, where it dominated the market, but nationwide.

Connie had prospered, against perceived odds, in this Texan "good ole boy" environment, taking to the creative challenge of attractively photographing products, laying them out on the page, writing compelling copy and subsequently maximizing the sales deriving from each mailed publication. Many companies were shy of what had always been regarded as an expensive way of generating sales. The cost of manufacturing and mailing a catalog was a significant expense, and measuring the responses and sales—the return on investment—was regarded as rarefied guesswork, rather than a science.

Connie had changed all that within Butterworth Catalogs. She had surprised her father by systematically attacking each element of the catalog production process and breaking it down into simple, repeatable actions. From the use of the studio where the products were laboriously photographed through the styling and use of models, Connie introduced strict time and cost guidelines for each photographic shoot, negotiating a fixed fee with the newly freelance creative teams and making them work through the night if necessary to complete their tasks. She persuaded her father to transfer the ownership of a vast, unused warehouse in the then distant and disregarded town of McKinney, northeast of Dallas. She converted the building to a state-of-the-art photographic studio with the space to store goods and clothing and create different display stages to match the seasons for each product shoot. It became a hyperefficient production line, and photographers complaining about the lack of creative freedom or tight deadlines were swiftly dropped from the roster. Those lensmen and stylists who remained became known as "Connie's Crew," and the freelance gig, if you were willing to take it on, was colloquially referred to as "The Perspiration Line," Connie having previously heard a stylist refer to the shoots as a sweatshop and, throwing one of her famous screaming tantrums, firing the poor girl on the spot.

She invited and then visited the printing companies that competed for her increasing volume of catalog work, cajoling them for lower prices on volume, then threatening them with taking the business away once she had established a short list of hungry suppliers anxious for the huge print runs that her merchant catalog clients provided.

Connie's final step in the supply chain was to ride roughshod over the printers' relationships with the paper suppliers too. The norm in the business was that the printer made the deal with the paper manufacturers for the supply of each job. On the face of it, this made economic sense—the printers were buying paper on behalf of a multitude of clients, and so economies of scale should mean that the printers could negotiate bulk buys and pass on those savings (or at least a portion of them) to their clients. These deals, to Connie's eyes, were cozy, mutually beneficial relationships that were to the detriment of the end customer—her. She had quickly figured out that the major cost for each catalog was paper and mailing. And due to the monopoly held by the United States Postal Service on the mailing element (something that she intended to tackle at a later date), her focus became quickly trained on the paper manufacturers themselves.

For her large catalog customers, starting with her father's business, she went directly to the paper providers, offering them long-term contracts based on a fixed price, something the paper companies had never done before, even with their largest printer clients. The paper business was a commodity-driven market, subject to large price swings driven by supply-and-demand surges as well as seasonal and climatic considerations. Connie offered to promote her chosen paper mills within the pages of her catalogs—she would prominently display "Your Butterworth catalog is printed on the finest International Paper in the world" on the inside cover of the publication, later adding words like "sustainable' and "managed forests" as she helped her industry favorites battle the growing environmental lobby.

Over the period of years during which she had taken the helm of Butterworth Catalogs, Connie single-mindedly attacked each facet of the production and supply chain processes, creating change, innovation and a scorched earth devastation of previously accepted norms and business practices. As a result, the cost of producing each catalog had come down, thus improving her profit margins and making the owners—now herself, as well as her father—wealthier. Her single-most celebrated achievement was to develop what she had named the "squinch model," a measurement system based on the sales per square inch of space devoted to each specific product in the catalog. Connie's focus on ruthless efficiency translated into measuring the effectiveness of every square inch of every page of every catalog. Her affectionate nickname among the staff—among a raft of much less affectionate nicknames, it had to be said—was Madame Squinch.

Her claim to have invented this model was hotly disputed by others in the industry, who repeated often that they had been doing it for years, but that didn't stop Connie from claiming it as her own, culminating in her being named as Executive of the Year by *Printers World Magazine*, Female CEO of the Year by *Texas Monthly* and number three in *Inc Magazine*'s 40 under 40. All this took place in 1999, the year that she became Connie Ross Butterworth and "changed lanes," as her husband, David, liked to say.

Connie Ross Butterworth, perched erectly at her window seat at her power table in the top power lunch spot in Dallas, in addition to being the "Catalog Queen of Texas," was now one of the most highly regarded (and some might say feared) executives in the world of public affairs.

"So, Connie," asked Walt Meyer, peering over his jumbo shrimp appetizer, "what can I do for you?"

Connie looked up at him from her garden salad. She saw a small globule of crimson cocktail sauce in the corner of his mouth that was about to separate and drop onto his plaid sports jacket, a jacket that had seen better days. She saw scattered specks of dandruff on the collar of that same jacket. She felt simultaneously glad to be out of the day-to-day of the catalog business, grateful to be living in Georgetown and largely absent from Dallas, apart from major social events, and happy that lunches with Walt Meyer were nowadays rare occurrences.

David had questioned her on the use of Meyer & Meyer for this transaction and counseled the hiring of a DC firm instead. But a few days ago, she had felt strongly about hiring Walter. "It's horses for courses," she had told her husband. "Besides, he knows the business inside out."

"We're goin' to sell the catalog business," she said.

"And you'd like us to handle the transaction for you?" A look of greed had quickly supplanted the initial surprise on Walt's face. The cocktail sauce made the transition from his bottom lip to his lapel. Walt didn't notice.

"I have a short list of companies for you to approach," said Connie. "I'm open to any others you can bring to the table."

"Of course, we'll be delighted to help."

"Of course. We'd also like your most favorable, favored-nation fee, please, Walter," Connie said, smiling tightly.

"Of course,"

Connie's thoughts suddenly cut to her now dementia-stricken father and how he would have done everything within his power to stop this potential transaction and to admonish her publicly for daring to suggest that a jewel in the Butterworth firmament could be offered up for sale.

"I'll send you our initial list. Our preference is for a trade buyer, Walter. Someone who will value the clients and the reputation of Butterworth."

"Do you think we might be off the peak for selling the catalog businesses?" ventured Walt, carefully, his tone neutral.

"Not at all," said Connie. "We are seein' a resurgence of print among the bigger retailers. Have you looked at your mailbox recently? And we have great new research on how print drives online commerce—it will all be in the package. I'll get it dropped off at your office this afternoon. If you can get us a draft prospectus and an agreement between ourselves as soon as possible, that would be wonderful."

Suddenly Connie was on her feet hugging a similarly coiffed and manicured female acquaintance. "Oh darlin'," she said. 'How wonderful to see you."

Walt rose and then sat back down, suddenly noticing the red splotch on his jacket out of the corner of his eye and wondering how quickly he could get out of there.

CHAPTER

SIX

"It's possibly not the best time to be away from the office," said Chris to Emily as they sat in the back of their Uber on the way from JFK Terminal 8 to downtown Manhattan.

"Um, probably not," said Emily, smiling and glad to be out of the maelstrom of the Brexit storm, if only for a few days.

"We just need to get the office set up and vet those freelancers for the pitch."

"And get the business registered, our name on the door, a bank account, some creative ideas, blah blah blah." Emily hadn't meant to sound overwhelmed; it had been meant as a joke, but coming out of her mouth after seven hours on a BA flight and a tedious wait at Immigration while Chris breezed through with his US passport, she sounded, as her father was fond of saying, a little less than gruntled.

Chris appeared to ignore both the tone and content and pressed on: "We have the attorney ready to go, Em."

He followed up, saying, "Don't worry about it. This is my neck of the woods. We like to get shit done in 'Merica," drawling out the final syllable with an ironic smirk.

Emily hadn't seen him this relaxed for weeks. The past months on the Leave campaign had been a relentless barrage of meetings, research, interviews and recriminations. Chris had been consistently good-humored and available to everyone within the agency. The creative team was burned out with being second-guessed by "a bunch of bureaucrats and second-rate pols," and the continual bickering at the client meetings had needed Chris's presence to be the "grown-up in the room," to use his words. Chris was particularly vexed by Boris Johnson, who was taking more and more of a prominent role in the meetings.

"He literally just makes stuff up," said Chris after one particularly fractious encounter. "He pulls numbers from thin air and then challenges you to call him a liar."

As the car emerged from the Midtown Tunnel close to the UN Headquarters, and the late afternoon sunlight streamed jaggedly between the Manhattan skyscrapers and through the dirty windshield illuminating the back seat. Emily looked across at the resting and ruggedly handsome features of her boss and felt a glow of pride. She was glad to be there, even if it had taken some juggling to get her now five-year-old, Justin, into a couple of sleepover nights with her mum and then with Brian's parents in Peckham. She'd had to provide a fabricated excuse to the nursery school, as well as give Brian some firm words about his role in the transportation and handovers. Brian's work hours were erratic, and she could also feel he was resentful of her trip to New York City, so she didn't push on his need to have Justin under the care of both sets of parents for a few days. Maybe the break would be beneficial, she thought to herself. Things had not been that great between the two of them recently.

They arrived at The NoMad Hotel, just off Madison Square Park (Chris's preferred location for the office space search), and having completed check-in, Chris motioned to Emily, saying, "I'm meeting someone for a drink at 6. Do you want to meet down here for dinner at 7:30?"

"Um, of course," she said, looking up from her phone, "but you should check your emails first. There's something in there you're not going to like."

Chris was huddled in the corner of the private bar at the rear of The NoMad Hotel. The lighting was low, and the setting was close to a ten on an "intimate lounge bar" scale. On the other side of the table from him was Randy Gardner, his US State Department contact, now clearly liberated from the confines of his London office. Randy, in shirtsleeves, his jacket folded neatly on the empty stool on the other side of the low table, leaned forward toward Chris.

A thick brown manila envelope lay between them on the red upholstered corner bench where they perched facing one another.

"It's all in there," said Chris, "apart from today's fiasco."

Randy picked up the envelope and weighed it in his hand.

"Meaty" he said. "What was today's development?"

"A big red bus," said Chris.

"Sounds intriguing . . ."

"Fucking Dominic Cummings," snorted Chris. "He and Boris cooked it up. It's a giant red bus that's going to tour the country. I don't mind the idea; in fact, it was one of ours—it's the giant billboard that it's carrying that's giving us heartburn. It reads 'We send the EU 350 million a week. Let's fund the NHS instead.'"

"Sounds like a powerful message," ventured Randy.

"Right. Except that it's total bullshit," answered Chris.

"He and Boris literally pulled the number out of their asses. Or arses, should I say? The UK doesn't send the EU 350 million a week, and there's no way any government is going to spend that on the National Health Service. Yes, apart from that, it's a powerful message, as you say!"

Chris was animated, his eyes bright with indignation.

"Presumably you have some legal vetting process in place?"

"Ironically, no," Chris answered. "The Advertising Standards Authority has no jurisdiction over political ads. Can you believe that? Basically, you can say anything you like in a political ad, everyone can complain and no one can do anything about it. So, that pork barrel Boris Johnson and sleazy Dominic Cummings sat down, and over the back of a napkin, they came up with a number, doubled it and, as the Brits like to say, Bob's your uncle."

"I've never really understood that phrase," said Randy. "But if you're going to lie, make it a big one, hey?"

Chris was nervous about saying any more, despite the fact that he was in a conversation with someone who technically didn't exist and who would never quote him to the outside world. His spymaster to be exact. Nevertheless, he had to acknowledge inwardly that the situation was pretty much all of his own making, as while, yes, it had been the agency's idea for the battle bus, it had been specifically Chris's. He'd wanted a red London double-decker, but a donor had offered the giant motor coach and been happy to have it painted red. The Leave team, particularly Boris, had leapt all over it. Ever the showman, Boris had half a dozen slogans within minutes. The quick math on how much Britain paid to the EU as a net contributor was quickly matched against where public opinion was most vehemently focused—the National Health Service, where standards had been declining for years, waiting lists for medical treatment had got ever longer and staff were desperately underpaid. The fact that many of the NHS doctors, nurses and support staff were from European countries was another inconvenient and overlooked fact that would be drowned out by the screaming typography. Boris had his headline, and his headline would be driving around the country on the side of a bright red battle bus.

"So, how's it going with the US Tourism folks?" asked Randy.

Chris quickly shifted gears. "Great!" he said. "We had a good first conference call. We're meeting with them the day after tomorrow at their offices in DC. We are seeing real estate in the morning for the office that's gonna be Intersect North America's New York–based HQ. They seem to like that we have an outsider's view of the US and are headed by a national." Chris emphasized this last comment by pointing an index finger at his own chest. "And I think they sounded pretty understanding when I told them we are going to need to staff up if we get their business."

Chris paused and then said, "I appreciate your help on this, Randy."

"No problem," said Randy. "We work with them from time to time; it's useful for us to have their name on our door in certain places around the world. I don't think they have huge budgets, but hopefully they should look good on your client list."

It was Randy's turn to pause and turn the subject back to Brexit. "Listen, your insights into the Leave campaign are proving pretty useful. Our prediction if the vote goes to leave The EU is that the PM will have to step down. Our reading is that David Cameron really did not expect the cards to be falling this way. The result is going to be mighty close, and your agency may be the difference makers. If Leave wins and Cameron steps down, the next Prime Minister of Great Britain is more than likely going to be one of the guys who's been sitting around your conference room table. Since you started sending us the tapes instead of the hard copies of the minutes, it's been a game changer for our analysis team. So, cheers!"

Randy Gardner, an unexpected new business source for The Intersect Agency, raised his glass to Chris.

Chris shifted uncomfortably. He'd asked Emily to start recording the meetings as soon as he realized the sheer volume of paperwork and the amount of "off the record" comments that weren't being captured in the minutes. Also, his claim to Emily that they needed to capture everything for history and posterity had an increasing ring of truth about it. The country had moved into an antagonistic mood, as the gravity of the impending referendum decision and the divisions between families, colleagues and friends were revealing themselves across dinner tables, coffee shops and bars in every community.

Chris glanced up as he saw Emily enter the bar from the discrete hotel-side entrance.

"Oops," he said to Randy, "it's my colleague from the agency, Emily Upchurch."

They both stood up as Emily approached.

"Emily, this is my friend Randy who made the introduction to the USTA."

"Oh, nice to meet you," said Emily. "I thought Chris had mentioned it was a contact in London. I didn't realize you were based here."

"I move around," said Randy, "and unfortunately, I'm just heading out to another meeting. Good to meet you, Emily."

"Oh, you don't have to leave on my account."

"Not at all. I'm already running late. Best of luck with the pitch, and maybe I'll see you again sometime." Randy hurriedly picked up his coat, glanced at Chris and shook his hand warmly, the iron grip having traveled the Atlantic Ocean intact.

"Well, sorry to scare him off," said Emily, not sorry.

"Not at all. He's been threatening to leave for the last ten minutes. Now what have I done to deserve to be escorted to dinner by such a veritable goddess?"

Despite herself, Emily could feel a blush rising from her neck as she felt the warm familiarity of Chris's hand on the small of her back guiding her toward the doorway from where she had just entered.

Although tired from the long day of travel, Emily quickly got her second wind as they left the hotel and walked through Madison Square Park. It was a warm spring evening, and the lights of the buildings surrounding the square and the elegant clock tower created a magical backdrop. It was Emily's first time in New York, and she had been trying hard all afternoon not to appear like an overwhelmed schoolgirl, but the view of the Flatiron Building as they came out of the park was too much for her:

"Oh my God, it's just like the films!" she gasped.

"The movies? Which one?" asked Chris

"All of them. The whole city. It's like every film and TV show you ever watched as a kid has suddenly come to life. It's just like I imagined, except bigger. And noisier!"

"It's how I felt about London the first time I went there," said Chris. "All those iconic sights are suddenly there in front of you in real life."

"*Home Alone* was our family favorite Christmas film," said Emily.

Chris laughed, "We'll see if we can swing by the Plaza Hotel tomorrow, although I can't guarantee we're going to be having any snow."

Emily giggled as they walked together in step toward the Gramercy Tavern.

She'd had a quick moment to look up the restaurant on her phone before leaving her hotel room to meet Chris. His assistant had handed her their itinerary before she left London, and she was intrigued and flattered to be included on most of the nonbusiness activities, although it had to be admitted, they were very few in number. The restaurant had looked super fancy and was frequented by a whole bunch of celebrities, by the look of it. She quietly wondered who they might see, tried to hide her excitement and also tried to remind herself that she wasn't on a date, just a business dinner with her boss.

The restaurant was everything Emily had hoped for—elegant, sophisticated and humming with energy and conversation. Chris was in his element, guiding her through the expensive menu and wine list with aplomb and without a trace of condescension. Emily was no stranger to good restaurants in London; she was a cornerstone presence at many client lunches and dinners at Chris's table at The Ivy. But dinner in New York City for the first time had nudged her out of her comfort zone, and Chris put her quickly at her ease as she glanced around to take it all in.

"So, what's the deal with Randy?" she asked, glass of Chardonnay in hand.

"Oh, he's just a contact at the State Department in London," he said quickly. "They have dealings with the Tourism folks around the world, and it turned out they were looking for a US agency of record when we chatted a few weeks ago."

"Oh, I wondered if you'd known him from here," said Emily. "A school friend or something."

Chris's earlier background in the States was a subject of much speculation within the agency, as he never talked about it, and it had become a more than occasional topic of gossip. He was a relentless name-dropper of his college and sporting contacts in the UK—and his stints at Oxford University and London Business School were trotted out regularly at media interviews and included on his bio slide at every new business presentation. It was well known that his father was a bigwig at GE and that there had been a very successful family business before then, but it was never part of any conversation with Chris. When he'd been interviewed by the trades, he briefly referred to his childhood growing up in Connecticut and then stressed his early desire to study in the UK at the oldest and best university in the world, Oxford. When asked about his family back in the US, Chris would mention "a couple of siblings" that he didn't see very often and move the conversation swiftly to other topics.

"No, Randy is just someone I met along the way," said Chris. "He's turned out to be a useful contact."

"Are you seeing any of your family while you're over?" ventured Emily, emboldened by half a glass of wine.

"I doubt that very much," said Chris. "They are all up in Connecticut, and I've no plans to be there this time."

"It's not that far, is it?" asked Emily. "It seems a shame if they live nearby."

There was a pause and silence from Chris. He picked up his napkin and brushed it across his lips. He seemed to be considering his next words carefully. "Em, we are not that close, to be honest. It's something I don't really like to talk about."

Chris folded the napkin back onto his lap and turned his full-wattage smile toward Emily, saying: "I'm rather the black sheep at the Crossley homestead and have been for a little while. Now let's talk through our presentation."

With that, the conversation was switched. Emily, feeling gently and charmingly reprimanded, quickly acquiesced to the change in subject, grateful for the genuine smile that accompanied it, and gathered her thoughts back into work mode as they waited for their meals to arrive.

CHAPTER

SEVEN

WASHINGTON, DC—JUNE 2016

"Connie, where the hell is my ASTA file?" bellowed David Ross, managing partner at RBA, a firm fully known, according to the brass nameplate on the door ten stories down on 17th Street NW, Washington DC, as Ross Butterworth Associates.

"It's where you left it, darlin'," speaking with her usual rasping drawl. "On your desk. Maybe under some other files?"

"No, it's not. Wait, maybe . . . OK, there it is," David McKenzie Ross, who customarily cut a striking figure, with his snow-white hair (longer than his wife liked it) but at this moment was featuring an oddly cut platform jutting out from the back of his head that no amount of cajoling or product seemed to be able to smooth into a streamlined hairstyle befitting a senior public affairs executive. The verging-on-elderly, tanned figure, with his somewhat mad scientist coif, found the errant file, tucked it under his arm and headed for the door.

"Where are you goin', darlin'?" asked Connie, looking up from her desk as he passed by her office.

"ASTA. It's our weekly meeting. I'm going to be late . . ."

"They pushed it back until this afternoon. They are runnin' their advertisin' pitch this mornin', remember?"

A momentary look of confusion crossed the face of David Ross.

"Did I get that memo? Oh, never mind. What time is the meeting? And when is Marcie coming back?"

"Yes. Three. And tomorrow," said Connie, trying desperately not to sound patronizing, nor twenty years younger than her husband—and patently failing on both counts.

David stopped in his march toward the reception area and turned right into Connie's office instead. It was an office styled for comfort, with deep-pile rugs, a couch against the wall and elegant lamps studded like sentries upon various expensive-looking pieces of dark brown furniture—small tables, bookcases, filing cabinets. Soft furnishings in stylish fabrics abounded, but the main feature of the office was that every surface, including Connie's large mahogany desk, was covered in large, mostly silver-framed photographs.

Connie's face featured in each one, her red hair prominent and catching the eye as if a small series of forest fires were breaking out, rectangle by rectangle, across the room. Connie with George Bush, Connie with Pavarotti, Connie with Willie Nelson, Connie with Nelson Mandela. Several of the photographs included David too, and these were either threesomes or group shots—associations maybe, perhaps party conventions. Prominently displayed on Connie's desk and oddly facing outward toward the door was a black and white photograph of Connie and David with an elderly Margaret Thatcher, a scrawled signature in the bottom right corner. Side by side was another photograph of similar size, also facing away from Connie's leather high-back chair, this time featuring a much younger Connie Butterworth, her hair a vibrant, curlier and more auburn shade of red and alongside the former Governor of Texas, Ann Richards. For the avoidance of doubt, the photograph had been autographed in a black sharpie—"To Connie—future Governor of Texas. Best Wishes, Ann Richards."

"What's that racket?" asked David, sitting himself down on the comfortable chair in front of Connie's desk.

"That racket is *Don Giovanni*, dear," replied Connie.

"Since when did you listen to opera at your desk?"

"Since Michael asked me to join the board of the Opera Society," replied Connie. "I believe in doin' my homework, as you know."

"How much is that going to cost us?" grumbled David.

"Not as much as your suite at the Redskins, I'm sure," replied Connie quickly. "And a lot more upliftin', I'm sure." Connie gave a throaty laugh and smiled at her husband.

"Are you coming to the ASTA meeting?" asked David, quickly moving the subject along.

"Yes, we are both goin', along with Patricia," said Connie. "I hate that they are goin' to be wastin' their money on advertising. Maybe we'll get an update."

"We should have thrown our hat into the ring," said David. "If they're chucking money around, it might as well be in this direction."

The truth was that Connie had been dismayed to hear that the US National Travel and Tourism Office had given ASTA both the brief and the budget to promote the US as a travel destination. The US Department of Commerce oversaw tourism, but the office was only there to provide statistics and advice. ASTA existed as an umbrella organization for the whole travel trade. The United States had never promoted itself as a travel destination, as it had never been seen as a government responsibility. It left that work to the airlines and travel operators, as well as to the individual states themselves. Most of all, the burden tended to fall on the tourist attractions. Disney probably spent more in a month than the US had spent on promoting itself as a tourist destination since the Revolution.

Connie had been mortified to hear from the Executive Chairman of ASTA that they had specifically been tasked to find an advertising firm to scatter government dollars around the world to promote the good ol' USA. The amount of money being spent around the world by Dubai, Croatia, Turkey, Singapore and others had gained the attention of the bureaucrats. Uncle Sam did not like to be outspent.

"We could definitely handle this for you, Zane," Connie had pitched the CEO of ASTA. "We know more about your organization and tourism than anyone else."

The CEO had been polite but firm: "We greatly appreciate everything that RBA does for us, Connie," he had said. "Your advice and representation on the Hill is invaluable, and we like you in that swim lane."

Connie had bridled at this last jab of jargon. She had prided herself, since she and David had teamed up professionally, shortly after they had gotten together personally, in specifically straying *outside* of the public affairs swim lane, often to David's discomfort.

Since they got together, her business instincts and David Ross's professional reputation had proved to be rocket fuel to the fortunes of the up-until-now, small, well-regarded firm. Connie's business savvy, charisma and energy had quadrupled the profits of the business within two years, and RBA had grown significantly since then. Now they had offices around the country, a commercial studio in Alexandria and a nascent media business in Atlanta. Connie anticipated the capital that they were about to raise through the sale of Butterworth Catalogs would enable them to further grow their empire and their influence—both within Washington DC and beyond. A big international ad campaign for Tourism USA would have been an excellent profile builder, both for her personally and for RBA, although most people increasingly now saw no distinction between those two entities.

At this very moment, over at the ASTA offices, Emily Upchurch was sitting in awe as her own charismatic boss was coming to the conclusion of his presentation. Chris was on his feet doing what he did best—being persuasive, charming and totally credible. Their two freelance creatives, Eric and Shawn, with whom they had rehearsed that morning, were also hanging on every word, as if hearing the proposal for the very first time. The small group of ASTA executives around the table were drawn into the same extraordinary bubble, as Chris boldly and vividly outlined the ideas that would transform the perception of the US as a tourist destination around the world.

He talked about a country with boundless and stunning geography—the forests, the lakes, the mountains, the oceans. He waxed eloquently about the history, the culture and the endless varieties of cuisine that the visitor could plunge into. Most of all he described an America beloved by the world through endless exposure to movies and TV shows over the decades—the New York skyline ("And yes, Emily, your very own Plaza Hotel," he had smiled at her, winking knowingly), the Hollywood sign, Harry and Sally's diner, the Miami coastline of Crockett and Tubbs, the ranches of *Gunsmoke*, even the Albuquerque neighborhoods of *Breaking Bad* and the downtown Baltimore of *The Wire*. These were memorized and, yes, beloved landscapes and scenes engrained in people's minds' eyes around the world. Folks, Santa Monica beach is real! All these iconic destinations can be visited on fewer dollars per day than if visiting Europe, plus the Disneys—Land and World—Niagara Falls, Yosemite, the giant Redwoods and Alcatraz!

"Europeans," Chris pointed out, as if revealing a mystical secret known only to him as an undercover American, "had an average *five* weeks of vacation; Japan—also blessed with leisure time and generous pay—was only seven hours from Hawaii; Frankfurt six hours from Boston." The passion, the facts and the imagery flew thick and fast from Chris Crossley's golden tonsils.

And critically, Chris wove his vision of an America presenting itself to the world with the persuasive voice of a homesick native son: "We Americans have no idea how much the world follows us and subliminally, secretly, knows and admires us. Now all we need to do is to tell them it's real, it's accessible and it's affordable."

It's Real. It's Accessible. It's Affordable.

The tagline appeared as a small, italicized jumble of words on the screen behind Chris before solidifying and growing, like a fast-moving jungle plant, into giant letters taking up the whole screen as the words were repeated from Chris's vocal chords, and a swelling soundtrack of "God Bless America" rose up as Chris delivered the punchline, which was the tagline.

He grinned broadly at the seated executives and bowed low in front of them, sweeping his arm across his chest and finishing the gesture by pointing at Emily: "Ladiees and Gentlemen—I give you the fabulous Emily Upchurch on keyboard, thank you very much!"

There was a pause around the table and the room as Chris concluded. A collective exhalation of breath and a return to reality followed. Chris had taken them to a movie through his words and delivery, and now that the lights had gone up and the reverie was over, the executives were anxious not to lose the moment.

"Thank you," said the CEO. "Very impressive!"

As they got their stuff together and bundled the laptop and the boards back into their cases and tubes, Emily squeezed Chris's arm tightly: "Well done, Boss."

Chris grinned broadly and locked eyes with Emily. "Thanks, Em. Couldn't have done it without you. Let's enjoy the rest of the day before we head back to Manhattan"

In the reception area, Connie, David and Patricia from RBA were seated, waiting, as the ASTA CEO and Intersect's pitch team came out of the internal door in a burst of animated chatter.

Connie's head jerked up, her long, elegant neck on a swivel.

The CEO shook hands, thanking each individual for coming: Chris, exuding charm and grace and smiling broadly; Emily, her dark hair tumbling forward over her shoulders looking like a fashion model in her yellow and somewhat revealing summer dress. The two creatives had dressed like twins in their skinny jeans, black tee shirts and boxy jean jackets.

Connie, her interest aroused by the activity in the reception area, immediately zeroed in on Chris. The effect on her was visceral and took her by surprise. Her stomach tightened, and she could feel the blood coursing through her veins. Now, that's a good-lookin' man, she thought to herself as she shifted in her seat. David Ross, normally an oblivious waiter in reception areas, noticed his wife's laser-like attention being directed across the room and followed her gaze with inward dismay.

The cobweb-cloaked sadness of being seventy years old settled over David Ross as he fought to keep his face and posture neutral. Here we go again, he said to himself as the thought settled within him like a rush of icy water.

Connie, her radar suddenly alerted, looked back toward her elderly husband, who had the look of a wounded puppy.

"And when you pulled out those visuals of the number of countries showing *Friends* on repeat. . . ," Emily enthused as she nursed her glass of champagne. She was at dinner with Chris and the two freelance guys, Eric and Shawn. They had decided not to get the train back to New York, as half an hour after they left the ASTA head office in Alexandria, the CEO had called them to say that the US Tourism account was theirs, providing everyone could agree to a suitable financial arrangement and if Intersect was able to confirm its team and its own US presence. Naturally, Chris had wanted to celebrate. He needed to get Eric and Shawn on board, and he and Emily needed to talk about hiring a full-time account manager.

The dinner was unfolding at Bourbon Steak Restaurant, where they had been able to snag a reservation as it was within the Four Seasons Hotel where Chris, on a winning whim, had decided he and Emily should stay the night. They'd need an early start, as the interviews for staff were set in New York next day, but wins had to be celebrated, and what better place to do it than a top DC restaurant within its leading luxury hotel?

As Eric and Shawn left to catch the last train, Emily stood up to give them a hug, now that they were part of the family, so to speak.

Emily excused herself to go to the ladies room. When she returned, she found Chris had ordered another bottle of wine and was surveying the dessert menu.

Chris looked at her, taking in the interest that men from different tables were discretely showing as she sashayed past them. Her looks had been described to him by a college friend as "Home Counties Beauty," meaning he supposed that she was a particular type of English rose. He really needed to look that phrase up, he decided. As Emily sat back down, Chris was entranced by the curve of her collar bone revealed by the neckline of the yellow summer dress and her flawless skin, noticing the faint pale down on her forearm as she picked up her glass. His eyes tracked the light flush on that skin rising up from her throat toward her graceful and beautiful face.

"Did you notice those three people waiting in reception when we left ASTA?" she asked Chris, seemingly oblivious to his gaze.

"The older guy, the woman with red hair and what looked like an account manager?"

"How could you tell she was an account manager?" laughed Emily.

"Because she was the only one not looking up and happened to be carrying the biggest briefcase," smiled Chris.

"Well, the couple are over there at the table in the corner," said Emily, motioning her head toward the front of the restaurant.

"How do you know they're a couple?" asked Chris. "He looks way older than her."

"And?" asked Emily.

"And nothing," replied Chris. "Just an observation. They must have had business with ASTA, I guess. They look like any other couple with nothing to say to each other," he said smiling.

"Well, they *look* like a power couple to me," said Emily. "Not that I'm an expert in the field," she grinned.

"I disagree, Miss Upchurch," smiled Chris. "If anyone was scouting this restaurant looking for power couples, they wouldn't go any further than this table, I can assure you!"

Emily blushed further; she wasn't sure what sort of compliment that was but knew by its delivery its intention to flatter. Chris sat upright opposite her, his athletic body alert, his blue eyes twinkling and holding her gaze with a directness that felt both revealing and reassuring. She was feeling quite buzzed; the excitement of the day, the success of the presentation, the heady and opulent nature of the surroundings and, most of all, Chris's now undivided attention had succeeded in spreading a warm glow within her. She had managed to snatch a quick conversation with her mum before Justin went to bed. Brian was out with his pool pals, and so they had exchanged text messages. She felt that she had tidied everyone over there away, so some harmless flirting with her boss would be the perfect end to a very good day.

Chris signed the bill with a flourish.

"Early start. Long day. Emily, I just want to thank you again for everything you've done on this trip and everything you do for Intersect. You are amazing, and I'm very lucky".

"Aw, shucks," Emily breathed, blushing profusely. "Isn't that how they say it over here?"

They walked together from the restaurant to the lobby.

"I also meant to tell you how stunning you look in that dress, Emily. That color suits you so well."

"Thank you, Chris, I appreciate the compliment."

They stood close together, waiting for the elevator, their arms touching slightly. Emily could feel the same electricity she had briefly felt in the Dog & Duck in London when their legs had been jammed together. It's a limb thing, she giggled to herself. She wondered whether Chris felt it too. She definitely felt giddy.

The doors to the elevator opened, and they stepped in together.

As the doors closed, Chris moved closer.

"Emily," he said thickly, "are you wearing any panties under that dress?"

She was surprised to not be panicking, and even more surprised that she was suddenly turned on. She made a quick decision.

"Yes, Chris. Why?"

"May I have them please?"

"What?"

"May I please have the pair of pitch-winning panties?"

"Now?"

Chris looked at her, smiling.

Emily handed Chris her purse, reached under her dress and slipped off her red lace thong over her shoes, one leg following the other as her shapely limbs stepped out of them.

She held out her hand to take back her purse and exchanged it for her underwear. Chris looked deeply into her eyes, held up the red lace to his mouth and nose and inhaled deeply.

The ping of the elevator announced that they were at their floor. The expense of booking two rooms was going to prove to be one too many Chris thought to himself as he steered his Head of Client Services down the corridor.

CHAPTER
EIGHT

"The newspapers are doing our job for us," said Chris to the assembled Vote Leave account team meeting over their Monday morning coffee and pastries.

He flashed up a montage of front-page stories on the screen behind him:

"BELEAVE in Britain," shouted the *Sun*.

"If you believe in Britain vote Leave," implored the *Daily Mail*.

Another slide showed a giant photograph of illegal migrants on the front page of the *Daily Mail*, which was accompanied by the headline "WE'RE FROM EUROPE—LET US IN!"

"And, by the way, I've lost count of the number of 'Independence Day' headlines," Chris commented bullishly as he flipped through the screen grabs. Finished scrolling, he asked, "Where's the Battle Bus today, Emily?"

Emily looked up from her laptop. Neither of them had mentioned their night in DC since their return from the US. Their continued warm connection the following morning and mutual declaration of "no regrets" had given way to business as usual on the return flight and then back in the office in Soho Square. Emily had been wracked with guilt when she got back home, but after a couple of days of increasingly fractious sparring with Brian, she started to reframe the evening as a celebration that went too far and an experience that still gave her butterflies as she remembered the night unfold.

"Trafalgar Square today, Chris. Boris in attendance," she replied brightly.

"Ah, the future Prime Minister and Admiral Nelson, what a combo!" exclaimed Chris.

The atmosphere in the room was not as upbeat as its leader, and sensing the mood, Chris asked: "So, people, what's the deal? What's on everyone's mind? Anyone?"

There was an uncomfortable silence. Chris was regarded as reliably approachable and usually hypersensitive to morale issues.

Eventually, Lars Petersen, a senior and well-respected figure in the business, broke the uncomfortable silence:

"Chris, I think we are all feeling worried about what's happening in the country. The anger, the, um, vitriol, if that's the right word. It's hard to watch. And I speak only for myself here . . ." Lars's voice trembled a little, and his underlying Nordic accent sounded slightly more pronounced. "But I can't help feel that we are partly responsible for all these high feelings. . . ," he tailed off, leaving the room hanging with the phrase "high feelings," which presumably suffered from an inadequately translated Swedish phrase that was weighing heavily on his mind.

"I know what you expect me to say," said Chris. "It's a national debate, and we are merely giving one side of the argument. But I get it. We're at a moment in history, and it feels like it's a little out of control."

There was a murmur of assent in the room.

"Here's my suggestion," said Chris. "It's different for me as I'm not British. Hell, I'm not even European, and I don't have a vote. Everyone who feels they need time to separate from the work before the vote next week can step down from the team. We're pretty much done with the meetings now anyway, and we can always get help from our bench if needed. You've all done an unbelievable job, and there are no hard feelings if you would like some breathing room. And consideration time."

Again, there was a pregnant silence in the room.

"You don't have to say anything now," said Chris. "Just let me or Emily know, and as I said, no hard feelings either way."

Another pause, and then Ed Vickers from the creative department put up his hand. "At the risk of sounding like a dick, do we still get our ten grand if we win?" he asked.

A collective and cathartic laugh bubbled up.

"Ah, the success fee," said Chris, also smiling. "If we help our clients achieve their objective, a win bonus will be distributed to everyone on the team. So, yes."

"But don't let that influence your vote," shouted Baz Bushell, Ed's boss.

The meeting broke up in a better humor than it had started.

Emily approached Chris at the front of the room as the others exited.

"Thank you, Chris. Well said."

"I know it's hard," said Chris. "I'm sure you have it going on with your family and friends."

"Too right," said Emily.

Emily leaned toward Chris, her face upturned and eager. Chris flinched and turned his gaze away toward his notes. Emily hesitated, wanting to say something but headed toward the door, hiding her disappointment—and hating herself for having to hold back tears.

Chris watched Emily walk away, knowing that he had, in that moment, needed to choose a pathway. The night in DC had been truly memorable and charged with long-held and never-to-be-for-gotten released sexual tension. The experience of Emily uncov-ered (and unleashed) had been everything he had imagined and more—and yet in the cold light of the days afterward, he had been surprised at the onset of what could only be described as a guilty conscience. A fling with an employee. A married employee. A married employee with a toddler. What had he been thinking? He hoped Emily had seen it as a one-off, a moment in time—and one not to be repeated. That genie now needed to go back in the bottle. Although having just seen the hurt in her doe brown eyes, he probably had some more road to run in that direction.

"What a shit show," said Randy Gardner later that day, echoing Chris's earlier sentiments. They were seated, as was now becoming customary, at a table for two in The Audley, a signature Victorian pub around the corner from the State Department outpost.

"They've divided the whole country. What a bunch . . . I don't mean your agency; I mean the politicians," Randy said hurriedly. "What possessed them to think that a referendum was a good idea? What's the point of electing a government if it won't make tough decisions? It was an act of craven cowardice."

Randy's rant and rhetorical questions were landing on an impassive Chris Crossley and ricocheting around the busy bar, unanswered but, by the sound of it, not undiscussed around and about the pub.

Chris had taken the long way to The Audley after leaving early from the office. He had wanted to see the billboards for the US Tourism ads that had just started appearing around the capital.

He'd managed to persuade the ASTA folks to take advantage of the situation in the UK to launch a test campaign, as in his view there was going to be a clamor to leave the country for a while whichever way the vote went. Unused to working so quickly, ASTA had signed off on a one-country test on a limited budget. Chris, in his usual way, had managed to cajole Mastercard into co-funding the campaign, thereby effectively doubling the advertising spend and allowing Intersect to start testing the work immediately. The Instagram posts were going viral, with the hashtag "Escape the madness" doing particularly well. The agency had already secured bookings for billboard space all over the capital for the Leave campaign. Now it was able to switch some of that real estate for the new Visit USA ads that sprouted like florid cactus blooms of color in the parched monochrome desert of name-calling slogans for "Leave" or "Remain" messages around the city.

The meanness of the political sloganeering on the poster sites was therefore contrasted by the giant vibrant pastel visuals of luscious US destinations close by and in some cases side by side on the billboards that sprawled on buildings and random empty spaces between those buildings around London. The Brits liked their word play, and so the creative guys had gone for simple headlines with movie or TV references that connected with specific destinations around the US.

Chris had taken a cab to Cromwell Road to see their ad placed at what was known as a "super site" due to its enormous size.

On a drab corner of a brick wall opposite a sprawling Tesco supermarket was a sumptuous shot of South Beach on which, in huge type, read "Miami. Nice."

The tagline underneath read "Escape the madness. Visit USA with Mastercard. Bring the passport of your choice."

As always, they had more executions than they had time or money to place them: "Things to do in Denver. New York State of Mind. La La Land. Viva Las Vegas—they were all simple and effective graphic treatments with lavish visuals of a country blessed with sunshine, sunny optimism and cultural affinity. Chris believed in the ads as completely as he believed in the business advertising. "Advertising is an underappreciated artform," he was wont to say to anyone who cared to listen.

The appearance of these ads at this time, in this specific week, provided a memorable counterpoint to the prevailing atmosphere of introspection and apprehension. Chris had come to see the Brits as a people who hated to take anything too seriously, particularly themselves, and the referendum was testing that light touch severely. Escapism was a powerful antidote to the grim realization that the upcoming national vote was not a rehearsal. And the US Tourism ads gave Chris the thrill that took some of the sting away from the sprawling, toxic Brexit campaign that had now turned into a mudslinging contest of gigantic proportions.

Randy had been looking at Chris, expecting a contribution to his rant, but it was clear that the CEO of The Intersect Agency was elsewhere. Chris had also been affected by the past few months, and the excitement of the win and the setting up of Intersect in the US had been his own counterbalance to the intensity and infighting of the Leave campaign. He was going to be glad when it was all over, and his private takeaway from the experience was that he was going to have to think twice in the future about taking on political work. Its poison worked its way deeply into the soul.

"How's the tourism thing working out?" asked Randy, changing the subject.

"Fine," said Chris. "I think this could be great for us on both sides of the pond. Thank you again."

Randy put up his hand, as if to push off the gratitude.

"You won it, fair and square. They were blown away by your energy and the ideas, apparently. We just made sure you were on their radar."

Randy picked up his pint and inclined his head to take a sip. Then looking up, he said, "Mind you, we apparently managed to piss off their public affairs agency. They thought they should have had the opportunity and made a big noise about it."

"Who are they?" asked Chris, only half-interested.

"They're called RBA—Ross Butterworth Associates. Influential in DC. He's a longtime lobbyist; she's the dynamo. David Ross and Connie Butterworth. Very striking. Her, not him."

Randy smiled.

"Oh," said Chris, his memory kicking in. "Redhead? Long neck?"

"I believe so. Did you meet her?"

"They were in reception after the pitch. And again in the restaurant later that same evening, apparently."

"She may be stalking you," chortled Randy. "Be careful. I hear she's a piece of work."

It was Chris's turn to smile.

Randy was more voluble than he'd ever been before, and the words continued to spill out of him: "She inherited her father's business in Dallas and seems to be selling it off piece by piece. The father's still alive, apparently, but not in good shape mentally, and she has power of attorney over the whole shebang. She married Ross a few years ago and took over his firm in the process. He had a solid reputation, but she's taken it to another level. Washington can be very rewarding for the ambitious."

"Speaking of ambition," said Chris, "how's it going for you at the State Department?"

Their relationship had assumed a somewhat jokey repartee over the past months as the volumes of transcripts from the Leave campaign meetings had landed in Randy's lap. Randy had confided that the tapes and reports had been disseminated around various corridors of power in DC and had given Randy's department a solid reputational boost, as well as given Randy himself a personal moment in the spotlight.

"Well, in all seriousness, Intersect has been an interesting case study for us," said Randy, assuming a slightly more formal tone. Safe to say that marketing agencies have now risen in our estimation as potentially valuable inside sources."

Chris grimaced slightly. "I guess I'm glad to hear it. I think I'll be sticking to advertising—the espionage business seems rather overrated. I'm not sure how often you're going to get a situation like this in the future. At least I hope we don't."

"True," said Randy. "I don't think any of us could have predicted that potential future heads of state would happily sit around a table for hours belittling each other about tampon taxes and battle buses."

"It's been a shit show," agreed Chris. "We'll be glad to get back to business as usual, although we'll miss the fees for sure."

"Roger that," said Randy. "It does make you wonder how they ran the world though."

Chris looked blankly at him.

"The Brits. The British Empire. Ruling the waves and all that. The pomposity and the misplaced arrogance. Honestly, how do they think they're going to survive on the world stage outside of Europe? I know, I've seen all your stats—the fifth-largest economy in the world? Give me a break. They're behind California and only just ahead of Texas. And they have 1% of their dentists—and it shows. Ha! Nobody's going to do them any favors when they're back on their own. They don't seem to get it. Trying to re-create a world that never existed."

Chris was startled. He hadn't expected such an outburst from Randy, who had always given off an even-keeled, seen-it-all, neutrality-is-my-watchword vibe with his careful approach, crisp white shirts and tasteful Brooks Brothers blazers.

Randy sensed Chris's alarm and continued: "You didn't expect that, did you? Truth is that I married into this sinking ship."

"What sinking ship is that?" asked Chris.

"The UK, Britain, Perfidious Albion. You're not the only American to go to college in the old country," he said. "Except I took the light blue option, instead of your sinister dark blue route."

"You did your degree at Cambridge?" asked Chris, surprised at his own surprise.

"Graduate degree. M Phil to be exact. Political thought and intellectual history. Two streams of inquiry that seem to be extinct right now."

A pause.

"Political thought and intellectual history. Got it,"said Chris.

"I met the love of my life at Cambridge," continued Randy. "We've been married for ten years, two kids. Maya's parents moved from India just after she was born; they're now British citizens, but you tend to see another side of the coin from their perspective."

"I can imagine," said Chris. "Most of my college mates were white and entitled, but we did have a guy from Fiji on the golf team at Oxford. Although I'm pretty sure Ben headed straight back there after graduation. He was not a big fan of the British weather."

"All I'm saying," said Randy "is that this self-deprecating, tolerant, good-natured, post-colonial bullshit is about as deep as the spray-painted Go Home graffiti on your garage wall. I'll grant you it's not just the Brits; it's happening all over. But this exercise has been very revealing if you happen to look and sound different from the average Joe." He paused and then went on, "To use a crass Americanism. Randy's eyes widened and rolled.

Chris weighed a half-full pint of London Pride in his hand: "I *do* get it. In fact, I get it all the time. What's the Churchill line? Two nations divided by a common language?"

"That's the one," said Randy.

"But in all honesty, I do think it has helped me with this project. To be American. They know, if I may use another crass

Americanism"—here Chris held up his fingers in imaginary quote marks and smiled—"that I don't have a dog in the fight."

"All I'm saying," Randy drained the rest of his glass, "is that the scars of this decision will run deep in this country."

CHAPTER
NINE

Connie Ross Butterworth was at her desk with a large sheet of paper in front of her, pen in hand, writing names around a large hand-drawn rectangle. She reached out to punch the intercom button on her desk phone. "David," she said, "are you OK with sittin' next to Senator Daley?"

"Judy Daley? Sure, but I probably need a Dem on the other side, right?"

"Yes, we're a bit short of Democrats tonight for some reason. They're either feelin' smug or worried about the election next week; I can't figure out which one." Connie's drawl stretched out the last word.

"So, a whole slate of pols. What clients do we have coming?" asked David.

"Jim from Exxon; Ryan from NRA; nobody on the health-care side; Zane, of course, from ASTA. He wouldn't miss a party for all the patent infringements in China." Connie gave a chuckle and said, "I still haven't forgiven him for not givin' us their advertising campaign."

"Let it go, Connie. They probably spent all of a hundred bucks. Their budgets are pathetic."

Connie released the intercom button. The election was days away, and these dinners were a civilized way of covering their bets. She had learned that a divided Congress was always best for business. David had schooled her well on the benefits of bipartisanship when she first came into the firm.

The now outgoing Obama administration had initially seemed a daunting prospect for most of their clients back in 2008, but with the Republicans controlling the House after his first couple of years and Obama's focus on healthcare, some of their worst fears on gun control (or gun safety, as they were calling it nowadays) and the environmental lobby had receded in parallel with the first deadlocked and then Republican-controlled Congress. The past few years had proved extremely profitable for RBA as they jockeyed to represent the interests of their clients on the Hill. Quite simply, the legislative impasse meant more meetings, more hours and more billings. Connie had quickly moved from believing in causes to believing in the *process* of government. Which all meant an ever-improving income for her and her husband.

When she had talked to her father about RBA and the way the business of lobbying worked, he'd been dismissive and hostile.

"That's the true definition of snake oil," he had snapped. "You're one step away from bribing them all."

"Daddy, it's the way Washington works," Connie had replied, hurt. "I'm just being a realist."

"A realist is a cynic who doesn't want to admit it," her father had replied, closing the conversation.

That was when he was cogent, remembered Connie, as she played around with her seating plan. Although even in his current state of deep dementia, she doubted her father would cut her any slack. He never had, and she reasoned it was one of the reasons for her success. Deep down it hurt, though—the constant cycle of trying to prove herself worthy; it would have been nice to have got at least one pat on the head.

"Patting on the head is what you do to horses," that gravelly voice always echoed in her head.

Connie glanced down at her schedule—she was juggling a lot, and the rest of the day was colored out in one- and two-hour segments right through to the hour before tonight's dinner. The upcoming Presidential election had the whole of DC vibrating with an undercurrent of palpable nervous excitement. A change of administration meant a new roll of the dice for everyone. The whole city would be affected, none more so than Washington's real-tors and moving companies as they jockeyed to find room for the incoming and swiftly switch out the unreturning and unelected.

Connie hit the intercom button again: "Darlin', I'm heading out for lunch shortly,"

"Remind me . . ."

"Walter Meyer and the guy from the advertising conglomer-ate. A gentleman called John Robins, I believe."

"Café Milano?"

"Of course."

"OK, see you later. I have a couple of meetings on the Hill this afternoon."

"Don't forget—dinner is at 7:30."

"I will not"

Connie released the intercom button, trying to rid herself of the nagging feeling of indifference and the increasing banality of their exchanges.

———

At Café Milano, Connie glided gracefully between tables, smiling and nodding. She could see Walt and the advertising guy rising to greet her as she approached. Lord, he *is* short was her first thought as she got to the table.

She extended her hand: "Connie Butterworth."

"John Robins, so pleased to meet you."

"Walter," Connie proffered her cheek and then gestured to the two men to be seated as she lowered herself into her chair between them.

———————

"So how was your lunch?" asked David Ross, as he struggled with his cufflinks at the entrance to his closet in the master bedroom of the Georgetown Ross Butterworth residence at 6:30 that evening.

"Oh, you know," said Connie, seated in front of the mirror of her dressing table close by and arranging her cascading dark red ringlets. "Interestin'. They want to buy the catalog business, and they also want to talk about RBA."

"What?"

"Relax, darlin'. I told him it wasn't for sale. And that it wasn't mine to sell."

There was an awkward pause between them.

"Why would they be interested in acquiring a lobbying firm, anyhow? asked David testily. "I thought they were in the advertising business."

"They're buyin' public affairs, PR, research firms. They see synergy, apparently," answered Connie brightly. "Don't worry, darlin'. I didn't discuss any numbers. I said I would talk to you and get back to him. He's preparin' an offer for Butterworth Catalogs. They see BC as essential to rampin' up their production services division."

"As long as they pay top dollar."

Connie was busy replaying the eventful lunch in her mind. John Robins, the CEO of Universal Holdings, had offered her not only a very generous multiple of profits or revenue for the purchase of her catalog business, but the chance to head up the whole division within Universal, join their board and take possession of an astronomical salary with stock in the parent company.

Connie had been prepared for an evasive dance at this, their first meeting. Instead, she had been on the receiving end of a stream of personal compliments, flattering descriptions of her achievements in making Butterworth Catalogs the absolute "pick of the litter," in Robins's estimation, and then a detailed and passionate explanation of Universal Holdings' strategy to completely shake up "the professional services" industry. Robins, who at first sight to Connie had appeared to be the archetypal accountant—short in stature, with short gray hair and short, bitten fingernails—had been everything but short in his vision for the future of his holding company.

He talked dismissively of the "mom and pops" that made up the majority of the creative services industries, he impressively ran through revenue estimates and percentage gains of whole sectors of businesses in which his acquisitions were thriving and, most tellingly for Connie, he had done his homework on the worldwide catalog sector. Excitingly for her, he shared her view of the continued importance of print catalogs in industries that most experts were predicting would consolidate into a digital-only world of e-commerce. She had been surprised when he had altered course in his breathless stream of facts and numbers to offer his take on the lobbying sector.

"Do you know how many political and bureaucratic decisions were taken in the last twenty-four months that directly affected our revenue forecasts for our advertising and PR businesses? One hundred and twenty-seven. And the revenue impact of those decisions—from trade embargos to regulatory details—was over $350 million. Imagine if we had half a dozen lobbying firms that were coordinating their activities with our PR and advertising interests?"

He had held up his hand at this point. "I know what you're going to say about client confidentiality and all of that stuff," he said.

Then leaning forward and lowering his voice, he continued, "But imagine . . . imagine if the daily reports from every one of these companies, with their myriads of clients, were all being rolled up . . . on a *daily basis* . . . into a report that landed on the desk of a couple of senior individuals. Those reports are incredibly well researched, written, synthesized and probability-scored. Yes, scored. What do you know about AI? Forget that—we'll come back to it. Imagine that a couple of senior individuals within the holding company were presented through these concise reports with the tools to act on and prioritize either the threats or the opportunities to UH overall and take immediate action."

Connie had attempted to interject, but Robins held up his hand: "Let me finish."

"And imagine that one of those senior executives was you. And that for every reversed negative impact and for every increased revenue decision on behalf of Universal Holdings, you were taking a piece of each and every dollar either saved or gained."

This short, animated, slightly overweight executive, with his cheeks of finely traced red and blue crosshatch veins and tufts of gray shrubbery protruding from his nostrils and shirt collar, had taken on an intense and hyperfocused air.

"First we achieve consolidation and scale in Production Services—that's where your catalog business comes in and you help us negotiate the best pricing in the industry while eliminating internal inefficiencies . . ."

"You'll be wantin' me to fire a few people then," smiled Connie.

John Robins pressed on, ignoring Connie's interjection:

"Then in the creative services area, we bring together teams to serve the individual clients but share the sector insights across every one of our businesses and ring-fence the teams so we can work for competitors in the different agencies."

"So, you're sayin' that the strategy team becomes a central resource for all agencies?" asked Connie.

"Exactly," said John Robins. "But not only that. It's also our research businesses, so it's a profit center, not a cost center. They would do the same for the lobbying firms. And of course, we have already centralized all the back-end functions—accounting, HR and the like."

Connie was listening intently.

Robins said, "We're going to pay you top dollar for Butterworth Catalogs, and we'd like to put you in charge of Production Services and let you run and right-size the operation. You'd quickly find a strong number two to oversee that division for you. Then we acquire RBA, and you work with me to structure the Universal Holdings Advisory Practice. We might go after one of the management consulting firms to inject some scale there."

Connie's mind was racing—this little man was on his way to assembling the most powerful creative and professional services businesses in the world, and here he was offering her the opportunity to play a significant part in it.

Breaking her train of thought, David Ross said, "Can you help me with these, please?" as he crossed the bedroom floor from his closet entrance toward Connie, a pair of cufflinks in his hand, his shirtsleeves dangling over his thin white wrists and hands.

"What are you thinking about?" he asked with a touch of tenderness and putting his hand on Connie's bare shoulder.

"Oh, just the dinner," said Connie, moving her shoulder slightly under his grasp to dislodge his hand. "Here, give me those cufflinks."

"In a couple of weeks, we may have our first female President," continued Connie, "if the polls are to be believed."

"I wouldn't bet the farm on it." David had backed away from Connie's dressing table and was heading back toward his closet. "That 'deplorables' comment of Hillary's may come back to haunt her."

Connie couldn't stop her explosion of fury: "Are you kiddin' me? After what that fool said about grabbin' women by the pussy? He's a complete ass! And an ignorant pig!"

"You can compare him to all the farmyard animals you want," replied David calmly, "but you of all people know it's a far higher bar for a woman, and there's a strong undercurrent running against the Washington insiders—or the swamp as he likes to call us."

"In any case," he added, "you grew up a Republican, so I wouldn't have seen you as rooting for the other side." David again kept his tone light.

"He's no Republican," Connie's voice had found a more even keel. "Besides, he knows nothing about politics."

"He's a streetfighter," said David. "An unlikely one, I'll grant you—and he has some pretty unpleasant people in his corner. All I'm saying is don't discount an upset. And be mindful of both outcomes over dinner."

"I know," said Connie. "You've taught me well. A divided Congress is a united bank account."

"Let's go downstairs. I can hear guests arriving."

CHAPTER

TEN

Chris was sweating now, the Seeburg 200 jukebox was glowing brighter and growing larger, filling up the room from the corner outward and toward him. The fluorescence in the jukebox was changing colors rapidly, the discs within the mechanism switching rapidly, playing a couple of bars of each song and then moving onto the next one before Chris could identify the track—sending out a cacophony of noise. Chris was horrified to see that the 45-rpm vinyl discs were being ejected from the machine, one by one; as they played, the discarded pieces turned molten as they fell to the carpeted floor, turning the beige carpet black.

Suddenly the room, which he had believed to be his office, had changed into a downtown bar. A feeling of nausea came over Chris; he was finding it difficult to breathe. Not that bar. Please. It was no use—the jukebox was now out of control, swelling like a balloon, filling the barroom in Darien, and pounding out music into a tune that was now becoming recognizable. A cracked version of "Jailhouse Rock" by Elvis. Chris was at the point where he knew he was dreaming and needed to leave, but at the same time his being was filled with dread—that track, what a cliché, that's ridiculous. I need to get out of here now. I can't breathe. And the fluorescent lights of the jukebox had now become the pulsating blue lights of multiple cop cars flashing through the windows, the revolving lights getting brighter and brighter matching the increasing volume of the music, which had changed again to Paul McCartney's "Band on the Run" . . .

Chris woke up with relief in his two-bedroom penthouse flat in Battersea. His bedsheets were soaked in sweat. He looked out of his bedroom window onto the shimmering silver brown surface of the River Thames. The morning light was beginning to seep up from the horizon with the eternal forgiveness of another day as his gaze swung east toward central London. It had been a particularly bad dream, this time more detailed and vivid than for a long while. He had briefly undergone therapy at the time, as requested by his parents, years ago now and just after the accident. The therapist had talked to him about the likelihood of such dreams, and she had been right; they'd stayed with him in various forms and always finished in a similar way—at the bar itself or in the ditch itself, always with the blue lights flashing, sometimes accompanied by sirens. As he shook this latest one off, he marveled at his brain's capacity for self-flagellation—the jukebox was an interesting new twist. He'd forgotten the details of the Connecticut bar where they had drunk beforehand, and yes, now come to think of it, there had definitely been a jukebox, although he was pretty certain that it wasn't a Seeburg 200. Now that *would* be ironic.

Chris got up and moved into the kitchen to make coffee, sloughing off the past and sorting through his upcoming weekend as he approached the espresso machine. Saturday was his true day of rest—and golf at Royal Mid Surrey with an Oxford pal and his friends was a highlight he looked forward to. He hadn't played much competitive golf since his days on the varsity team, but he relished the fact that most of his British friends wanted to play seriously and for money—it brought a more focused and more satisfying edge to a round, particularly if he was pocketing the winnings, which was almost inevitably the case.

Somehow he had talked himself into a date later that evening, someone he'd met at an industry awards dinner a few weeks earlier; and in a fit of sudden enthusiasm after a flurry of text messages, he'd found himself responding in the affirmative to a series of flirty emojis. He had stayed away from the dating scene for a few months after his night in DC with Emily Upchurch. He still had difficulty processing that evening, knowing that he'd instigated it and knowing he'd crossed all boundaries of behavior he thought he'd set himself. He found it difficult to be in her presence now, the familiar and stirring lines of her body as he watched her move around the agency floor, her long dark hair falling across her face as she leaned forward to speak and the faint pink of blush around her throat when she sensed he was looking at her. He'd made that decision when they got back to London that there should never be a repeat, and while it was probably frustrating for her that they hadn't talked about the night, it was surely better for both of them—especially with her being married and with a child, he reasoned—that the night should be cherished in each of their memories and then deeply buried.

His phone pinged the arrival of a text message from Randy Gardner: "Sry 2 bug u on wknd. Ru around 2 meet tmrw? Something big."

Chris smiled inwardly—Randy thought he was so cool with his abbreviations, presumably assuming that Chris was at the cutting edge of communications because of his job and would appreciate the brevity and street cred. They used a messaging app approved by the State Department, and Chris assumed they weren't being charged by the character so it always amused him when Randy's tortuous messages, some of which would challenge a professional codebreaker, activated his mobile screen.

"Sure. Lunch?" Chris replied.

Sunday was usually his day for catch-up at the office in any case. He liked to spend time re-reading the memos he skipped through during the week, as well as planning and writing up critiques of existing work, ideas for new campaigns and long, pointed suggestions to the new business team on potential clients for the agency. In addition, the New York office was proving to be a particular time suck. He didn't have a reliable senior person in place yet, and Emily was overseeing the client service function from London—a situation that really couldn't continue for much longer. He needed to spend a couple of weeks in the States and was planning to get over there as soon as possible.

He would get those plans in place during Sunday, and he'd treat himself and Randy to a good roast lunch somewhere in town. Again, Chris was amused with himself. He had turned into one of *them*, he thought. Only a local referred to London as "town," and only a Brit would be yearning for roast beef, roast potatoes and Yorkshire pudding on a Sunday lunchtime. He really needed to get back over the pond and spend some time reacclimating himself to his native land.

His phone beeped again with another text: "Chris, if this is still your cell, please call me. Your father is not well. Mom."

Chris's heart sank. He had not heard from his mother in a couple of years, nor from his father in ten. It had to be today of all days, he thought to himself. He was still rattled from his night of broken sleep, and it was feeling like a conspiracy of the universe. He texted quickly back: "I'll call you later."

He didn't know how much time he would buy, but he needed to regroup. Whatever it was, it couldn't be that serious, he reasoned. "Not well" did not, in his view, mean seriously ill—and whatever the ailment, she would have surely put "had a stroke" or "suffered a heart attack" if the situation were super urgent. There were too many complicated feelings to unravel for him to jump on a call with her immediately, and now he was realizing that it was 5 am on the East Coast, making him feel even more conflicted. Had she woken up and hit send on a message she'd been sleeping on? Or had she been up all night with an ill husband and decided to guilt his estranged son through sheer exhaustion and annoyance?

Either way it could wait a couple of hours, and he would call from the golf club, that way avoiding any protracted or potentially emotional exchange.

———————————

The "Sunday morning Chris Crossley" was definitely a good version of himself he mused as he sat at his desk in a virtually empty office building. Basking in an excellent win on the golf course and an enjoyable first date the night before, Chris was shuffling through his paperwork and deleting emails like a man on a mission. The golf game had come down to the final hole, and his pitching wedge to three feet had sealed the win and £50. The evening following had been fun from the outset. He had put out of his head until half an hour before they met in Chelsea that his date was named Emily. Emily Smith had been on the judging panel at the Advertising Awards dinner, and Chris, as both recipient on behalf of the agency and, these days, a frequenter of top tables at industry events due to Intersect's currently sky-high profile after the Brexit win, had been seated on one side of her. Their conversation that night had been light and flirtatious. He hadn't learned much about her personal life, and so most of the conversation had been business-related. This Emily was a high-profile marketing executive for the National Lottery and an articulate industry advocate of ethical digital marketing.

Their date had revealed her to be a lover of good food, widely traveled and an enthusiast of music from the 1980s. Thus, they had found themselves dancing the night away at Maggie's—a club on Fulham Road dedicated to 1980s music where Emily had shared that she was currently separated from her husband of almost ten years and was just looking to enjoy herself while they pondered their respective futures. For Chris's part he was grateful to be in vivacious female company and to finish his Saturday on a high. They had parted ways in the early hours of Sunday morning, promising to get together again in the near future, after some shared chemistry on the dance floor and in the back of the cab to drop Emily just down the road in Fulham.

His conversation with his mother from the Royal Mid Surrey clubhouse had been the low point of the previous day. Chris mulled over the information that his father had suffered a heavy fall, reason as yet unknown, and had broken his hip. His mother had wanted to let him know and had taken the opportunity to again try to persuade Chris to offer up an olive branch to address the long, and so far, intractable breach in the Crossley family. Chris had been firm that the ball still lay in his father's court, broken hip or not, and that he was not about to try to mend the unmendable, end of story. Chris's mother revealed that his father had read about the success of the Leave campaign in the *New York Times* and of his son's role in leading the advertising approach to the momentous and historical event of Britain leaving the EU.

"And?" Chris had asked.

"Well, just that he noticed," said his mother, before adding, "And he was proud."

"Did he actually say that, or is that you editorializing?" Chris had said sarcastically.

His mother had gone silent as another chance to heal long open wounds appeared to have slipped by.

Chris was skimming through his senior staff's email accounts by now, as lunchtime approached. Randy had agreed to meet him at Simpsons-in-the-Strand for his Sunday roast, the quintessential old-school restaurant for those in search of the British dining experience of the culinary wasteland era of London dining, according to some but not to Chris, who relished the terribly English, white tablecloth, rude waiter vibe.

Meanwhile, this chief executive of one of London's top up-and-coming advertising agencies was sifting through the email accounts of his employees. Chris had set up access long ago when the business was in its infancy and there was rampant paranoia about breakaway groups of senior employees leveraging client relationships to set up their own businesses. Since then, the lawyers had schooled the sector in employment contracts with punitive noncompete clauses, and the agencies themselves had got more generous with profit sharing and other participation schemes. But Chris remained on alert for any signs of collusion and potential plotting and had become accustomed to keeping an eye on his senior folks' communications. He also marveled at how people used their work email addresses for all the messy personal details of their home lives. He reasoned that he was protecting his business, not snooping, even as he absorbed the back and forth between Baz Bushell and his boyfriend and the recriminations following a recent weekend in Brighton. He scanned Emily's outbox too, less in fear of any work improprieties, as he trusted her completely, but more in search of any clues of the relationship between her and her husband. But unlike many of the other senior personnel in the business, Emily scrupulously kept her private life correspondence out of the work email environment. Chris scrolled through looking for any indication as to how she felt about her life and more specifically him, but there was nothing there to give him hope, if that's what he was looking for.

He didn't really know what he was searching for if he was honest with himself. His life revolved entirely around his business.

He lived it all day, every day. It consumed him entirely, and if he were being filmed at that moment for a documentary, the camera would pan out from him hunched over his computer forensically examining his staff's emails to the wider shot of his perfectly curated ad exec office, pausing knowingly on his McCartney-inherited jukebox in the corner, and then out through the window looking back wistfully at the figure alone at his desk in an empty building, while quickly moving attention to the busy Sunday morning comings and goings of the regular people with more balanced lives strolling through Soho Square.

"So, where do you stand on guns?" asked Randy, chewing cautiously on what he felt was meat gristle, but could have been what the Brits regarded as prime roast beef. "More specifically, before you answer that, where do you stand on the Second Amendment?"

Randy had given up home-cooked lamb korma for this meeting and was determined to get a clear read on what he regarded as a potentially risky escalation of the use of Chris Crossley as an asset to the government. He'd already expressed some misgivings, but the introduction of the US Treasury to the case study he'd submitted on the success of the insights gained by the State Department's sponsorship of the Intersect/Brexit infiltration had opened the door to a potential new assignment. Randy's generous introduction and leg up for Intersect's New York presence had also tipped the scales somewhat—the next quid pro quo was now considered to be due on Chris Crossley's side of the ledger by the department. It had not gone unnoticed that the US Tourism business had quickly attracted critical notice, and a small but growing stream of new clients for the agency whose London reputation as a "hot shop" had done it no harm in the gray corporate sameness of the Madison Avenue advertising world.

"So, there it is," thought Chris as he too struggled to swallow a lump of overdone meat drenched in a gravy that was slowly coagulating on his plate alongside some limp Brussels sprouts and a giant Yorkshire pudding. He'd wondered whether the success of the collaboration with the State Department would be a gateway drug to other opportunities, and so here we are. This spying game is a somewhat drab and predictable business, he thought to himself.

"I haven't given it much thought recently," said Chris, "It's not really high up on the agenda over here, is it?"

"I'm talking about the US context, naturally," said Randy, slightly impatiently. "The right to bear arms?"

"A well regulated militia, being necessary to the security of a free state, the right of the people to keep and bear arms shall not be infringed. That one," said Randy.

"I guess I'm for it in principle," replied Chris. "I am also in favor of the regulation part of it."

"Well, I guess that's OK," replied Randy cautiously, "depending on what you mean by regulation. Let me explain a little—bear with me."

"The National Rifle Association was formed in 1871 to advance the excellence of rifle marksmanship. And it pretty much stayed that way until nearly a century later, in the 1970s, when the NRA changed its course—and cause—to become much more of a lobbying organization. It went about raising a lot of money to defend the Second Amendment, which it felt was vulnerable. It also aligned itself with the Republican Party, where it has stayed. It's now one of the most powerful lobbies in the country," Randy paused, letting the words sink in, and then added, "That's the very short version."

"I know a little about the NRA," said Chris. "What's this all about, Randy?"

"Patience, Grasshopper," smiled Randy, folding his long arms across his upper body and leaving his plate of beige food to look after itself. "So, if you remember, after 9/11, the US government created the Department of Homeland Security to safeguard the country against future attacks and threats?"

"Um, sure."

"The State Department is a strong partner with the DHS in our role as gatherers of intelligence around the world to help them make assessments to inform their activities," continued Randy. "We provide the Department of Homeland Security with plenty of ground intelligence from around the world to support their mission in the US, and we are not the only network doing so. Back in the US—and bear with me here, Chris, because it gets a little complicated—one of the roles of the DHS is to combat terrorism threats, both foreign and domestic."

"Got it," said Chris, a little impatiently as he watched Randy choose his words carefully and deliver them with great care, as if reading a book to a four-year-old.

"When it comes specifically to domestic terrorism threats, the DHS is seeing an uptick of activity, with the current administration being perceived as, how shall I put this? Let's say, a little less hostile toward some of the groups that we are keeping a close eye on. Since the DHS has only been active for fifteen years or so, as you can imagine, as we live in a relatively complicated organizational bureaucracy, there are some overlapping responsibilities in this area. All this is to say that there is a division of the US Treasury that also has responsibility for overseeing domestic terrorism threats."

"The US Treasury?" said Chris. "The IRS is in charge of hunting down neo-Nazi groups?"

"Well, you're not entirely wrong. You know the expression "Follow the money"?" Randy asked.

"It's a bit of a credo for me," Chris said, allowing himself a wry grin.

Randy explained, "It is the optimum way of infiltrating and uncovering terrorism networks, foreign and domestic. Financing these activities is a key vulnerability for them all, and keeping financial transactions away from the scrutiny of the authorities is one of their biggest challenges. It's one of the reasons behind the recent and rapid rise of cryptocurrencies, for example."

Chris had last seen this level of intensity in Randy when he had his first meeting over a year ago in Farm Street.

"There is a special division within the Treasury Department," said Randy, "and I've been walking them through our relationship with you and Intersect and how we were able to leverage your access to the senior leadership of this country at the time of the referendum campaign. They are intrigued about the opportunity of using a marketing agency to gain inside information without the risk of an undercover operation."

Chris digested this. He didn't like to hear his role described in these unambiguous terms. In his mind, he had merely shared some internal memos that had no bearing on the result of the Brexit campaign. The fact of the matter, he was beginning to realize, was that he was now firmly and inextricably linked with secret US information-gathering efforts. He had allowed himself to be lulled into a sense of false security, as no one had asked for any feedback or reports on the Tourism account, so he had let both the source of the business and the reason for its being there fade from his mind. The deal had been a business deal—who remembers all the conversations, confidences and favors that get you there? Whatever Randy was about to unveil had the uneasy feel of a noose tightening, but he couldn't tell why or how as yet.

"We can get into the detail down the road," said Randy. "The broad strokes are that we, and as I say, the 'we' in this case is a division within US Treasury, may have the chance to put Intersect in front of the NRA. Treasury is considering putting all their marketing and communications out to tender. We collectively sense an opportunity to get better insight into the way the NRA may be facilitating pricing and access to their manufacturing partners and donors."

"What does all that mean?" asked Chris carefully.

"I need to be careful here," said Randy, "and you need to cast your mind back to the confidentiality papers you signed."

"Got it."

"The NRA seems to have suddenly gotten emboldened by the unexpected arrival of the Trump administration. They and the gun lobby generally had been preparing for a Hillary presidency. At the same time, we believe that the NRA leadership has become even more, er, how shall I put it, self-serving? And as I said just now, if they are actively facilitating access and preferred pricing to domestic organizations that could be classified as threats to our democracy, then that's a big no-no. We see having a marketing agency on the inside of the NRA as a way of getting better information. We know that some of the tradeoffs for either money or equipment—and in this case 'equipment' is the word for firearms—is promotional spend."

"So you think the National Rifle Association is funding right-wing militant groups under the guise of its marketing budgets," Chris said out loud, causing Randy to grimace and glance quickly around the room. Luckily, the tables were far apart, and the other diners seemed to consist mainly of elderly men focused on their meals or loudly conducting their own conversations.

The waiter approached their table, observing the half-empty plates and cocking his head. "Everything orl right, gents?" he asked.

"Fine, thank you," said Chris. "Eyes bigger than our stomachs . . ."

"No problem. Now, what can I get yer—sticky toffee pudding . . . or spotted dick and custard?"

Randy stifled a snort. "I think we're fine."

The waiter quickly disappeared, undoubtedly thinking, if not actually muttering, something about bloody Yanks.

Randy exploded: "Gets me every time. How does he say the words 'spotted dick' fifty times a day with a straight face?"

"He's obviously had some practice, I guess. . . ," said Chris, whose mind was elsewhere. "So . . . what is it that you want me to do about this NRA situation? We've only been up and running in the US for a year. It's going to be a stretch to make a short list with that size of a client, however well we're doing."

"We're working on that," said Randy. "Homeland Security has someone on the inside of the NRA, not sure where exactly. Do you remember that lobbying firm in DC that was pissed about you winning the tourism account?"

"Yeah, vaguely," said Chris. "Why?"

"Ross Butterworth Associates. The NRA is one of its biggest pieces of business. There might be a way in through them. We're looking at that angle too."

Chris had a sense of foreboding. This did not currently sound like a well-thought-through plan. Although he had enough self-knowledge to realize that his ambition currently knew no bounds, and much as he could look at himself somewhat critically, he knew he would remain open to the business opportunity. He had to imagine that the NRA spend was in the tens of millions of dollars, and that would make a significant impact on Intersect's business both in the US and across the whole company.

As he digested the conversation of the past ten minutes, he had come to the realization that at heart, these days he was probably not such a great gun advocate as he would be needing to appear to Randy. This was somewhat of a revelation to Chris. He had been in the UK for a long while now, and he had obviously got used to the absence of guns. The police rarely carried them, except at airports, and the UK news had been mercifully free for a long time of the grim routine that enveloped his home country every few weeks—reporting on yet another mass shooting and the consequent empty rhetoric and wringing of hands that ensued.

He knew Britain had endured its own school shooting massacre back in 1996, which had resulted in the national banning of handguns and a massive buyback program to remove them from private ownership. He was often asked in conversation why the US continued to do nothing to prevent these repetitive tragedies, and when his home state of Connecticut had suffered the most horrific elementary school massacre at Sandy Hook a few years previously, he remembered that he had struggled mightily to articulate a defense of his home country's rampant gun culture.

"Well, I just wanted to give you a heads-up," said Randy, interrupting Chris's train of thought. "Have a think about it. We're going to need to move quickly, so if you have any thoughts or contacts, let me know. We'll be back in touch early this week."

Randy looked over his shoulder to try and catch the eye of their absent waiter. Then he said with a chortle, "He's obviously running around the kitchen looking for spotted dicks," as he reached for his inside jacket pocket for his wallet.

Chris raised his hand. "My treat," he said, the metallic taste of the gravy coating the inside of his mouth, signaling that Simpson's may have fallen off the Crossley short list, or maybe it had been the conversational topic that had caused him to lose his appetite.

CHAPTER
ELEVEN

This meeting was turning awkward. Intersect's executive team was assembled in Chris's office, arranged around the small conference table that sat in front of the jukebox. Emily Upchurch, Head of Client Services; Baz Bushell, Chief Creative Officer; Lars Petersen, Head of Strategy; Laura James, who was transitioning from heading up Production Services to leading a newly reconstituted Human Resources function; and David Davies, Chris's longtime Chief Financial Officer and former Oxford classmate all sat hunched around the small glass-topped table, precariously balancing laptops and notepads.

Emily was speaking forthrightly: "All I'm saying is that if you are going to be spending more time in New York, we need a formal management structure here, Chris. We have onboarded three major new accounts in the last couple of months, and we simply don't have enough people. I know Laura is doing her best to recruit, but she's also carrying her production responsibility, and there are not enough hours in the day."

Lars weighed in: "This is correct, Chris." Lars, speaking in his heavy Scandinavian accent, enunciated carefully as he added, "We are running out of freelance strategists, and the media department really needs more help."

"OK, I hear you," said Chris. "But these are good problems to have, right, Dai?" Chris looked imploringly over toward David Davies, who was more familiarly known as "Dai" Davies, Dai being the Welsh diminutive of David.

Dai had been an outstanding rugby player at Oxford, and both he and Chris had become instantly friendly at Keble College as freshmen. Both excelled as athletes at their own sports, and both had been considered outsiders—an American and a Welshman—who had bonded while the predominantly English and public school ("public school" being the British euphemism for private school, as Chris quickly found out) crowd swam laps in their own gene pool and bantered among themselves in their own posh lingua franca. At first, Chris, from the preppy suburbs of Connecticut, had been a closer fit to the Keble crowd than Davies, an outsized and awkward youth from west Wales. And Chris had been the cultural emollient that had allowed both athletes to be accepted by their peers after the short but necessary initiation rituals that the tribal nature of freshman Oxford college life required.

"Yes, the numbers are outstanding," said Davies. "We're set for a record year, absolutely." This was the usual length of a Dai Davies conversational contribution.

"Which means record bonuses," added Chris.

"Yeah well, there might not be that many more years of Intersect if all these new clients join and then leave," chimed in Baz Bushell, his harsh Cockney accent cutting through the air as an antithesis to the lilting tones of the CFO. "We're in the same boat in creative. We can't hire fast enough."

"I'll be able to put more time into the London office now that you don't need me in New York," said Emily, sliding in her comment like a stiletto.

"It's not that I don't need you, Emily," said Chris quickly. "This office is our priority, and you have the heaviest weight of responsibility with the new clients in London. I need your focus here. I'll be in New York, and it will fall to me to get a team structure in place as well as getting our pitch team together. I think I should be able to manage that on my own."

"Fine. Rebecca should be able to manage the US Tourism stuff with a bit of my help from here," said Emily. "She's super young, but she's done pretty well so far. Plus, the client likes her. I'm sure you can manage it. My point is that with you gone, we'll need a more transparent chain of command here . . ."

A silent pause settled around the room. The uncomfortable exchange was like hearing your parents arguing at the kitchen table. It was unusual for Emily to voice such strong opinions, particularly in front of the executive team. She was seen by the others as Chris's reliable and loyal back-up and was not one to prolong a public discussion that could easily be solved in private between them.

"Dai is the most senior representative of the London office in my absence," Chris said carefully. "But this is a senior *team*; we work together. You are all heads of your own disciplines, and that won't change when I'm in New York. Which, by the way, is an email or a text message away. I know we're suffering from our own success right now, but we all know the market. When you're hot, you're hot, and we have to take advantage of that. And . . . ," here Chris leaned forward and raised his voice quivering with passion, "not only are we hot—we're on *fire*."

Chris finished with a double hand gesture of a large explosion and a huge grin, his face animated, eyes shining. They'd all experienced the pitch Chris, the persuasive Chris, the frontman Chris, and here he suddenly appeared, imploring this audience, his handpicked team, to believe. To buy. It was his trademark move, and it worked. The group acquiesced with a collective snort or laugh or smile. All except Emily, who remained still and impassive, her face bowed somewhat but not submissively, her neck edged in a light pink flush and her full lips compressed.

"You're right," she said, looking fiercely at Chris. "We *are* the cool kids in town, and there *are* a shit ton of people wanting to join us, employees as well as clients. All I'm saying is that we need better processes and a faster conveyor belt." She smiled tightly and looked slowly around the table, face to face. "I'm sure Dai can help us fast-track some of the organizational stuff—contracts, computers, space. And I know Laura's just taking this on, but we need these people trained in the way of Intersect, what we stand for, how we do things. All the vision, mission, purpose stuff we agreed on weeks ago. We are only as good as the people we hire." It didn't feel like an accident that as she finished her sentence she was again looking directly at Chris.

There was a collective affirmative noise and general nodding around the table.

"Agreed," said Chris, relieved. "I think most of those meetings are in the diary-slash-calendar over the next day or so." Chris's knack of showing his fluency in British and American office-speak was a show of strength as well as a mood lightener.

"Are we going to talk about the US opportunity?" Emily asked. The color around her neck had darkened slightly. It was clear that the meeting wasn't over from her point of view.

"Well, it's early days, Em," said Chris. "We're still figuring out whether we are on a pitch list on our own or in collaboration with another agency, and we're a long way from knowing the brief, let alone whether we end up winning anything."

"I mean, are we going to talk about what they do?" replied Emily. "And what that does for our reputation? And whether we are morally comfortable with the National Rifle Association as an Intersect client?"

It was Chris's turn to color. "First, as I said—we don't even know if we're on a pitch list. Second, they are the most powerful trade association in the US. And third, we have this thing in the United States called the Second Amendment—*and . . .*"—Chris's handsome features were momentarily coarsened and lessened by his sneering look and the ensuing tone of sarcasm—"the Second Amendment is preceded, believe it or not, by a clause known as, wait for it, the First Amendment. Which, if anyone is not aware, guarantees the right to free speech. And we as an agency support the right to free speech." Clearly angry, chin jutting forward, Chris looked from face to face around the table, challenging the next voice.

Which, again, was Emily.

"When we finished with the Brexit business, we agreed to focus on commercial clients and to be very careful about taking on a political cause again." Emily's voice was quiet and firm. "I do understand that the Leave Europe campaign put us on the map, but the issue not only divided the country; it also divided the agency. Guns are an even more divisive issue, don't you think? I'm just asking—are you sure we want to take this on?"

Chris did his best to hold himself in check. He looked around the table at his executive team. "Anyone else?" he asked tersely.

The right hand of Baz Bushell went up.

Baz had been with Intersect for three years—he'd been a big hire for the agency, and Chris had approached him after Baz had been showered with awards for his work on the Mini Cooper account with his previous agency. Baz's award-winning campaign there had been a pastiche on the movie *The Italian Job* and had caught the eye with its high production values and use of humor to promote an iconic British brand that drew attention away from the fact that Mini was nowadays a mini-BMW and German-owned. The "British Job" Mini commercials had entered the popular consciousness—and in fact had been reused by Intersect during the Leave campaign. The Mini Cooper catchphrase—"It's just the job, innit?"—had carried exactly the right amount of on-point London slang, redolent of Michael Caine from the original movie and tinged with a general irreverence to lodge itself back into the argot of the viewing public. Leave Europe had taken on the cultural inheritance of an iconic British brand separating itself from its recent European encumbrance. It had been a smart and successful addition to the campaign, and Baz had been lauded for it a second time around.

"Em's right, Chris. This might not play well for us over here. Since Dunblane, there's been a hard public opinion against guns. We don't like 'em! And to be honest, it's the biggest single issue that makes us Brits more civilized than you Yanks—we stopped shooting schoolkids a couple of decades ago."

Baz always delivered his words with a smile. It was a natural part of his character, and with his strong London accent and patter, he played the cheeky Cockney persona to the full when it suited him. The technique worked for him, as it lessened the shock of his blunt, often crude observations, one of which he had just delivered at the table.

Chris, who had still been in attack mode when Emily had stopped speaking, gave Baz his full attention, mindful of his Creative Director's recent successes and current sky-high reputation in the industry.

And while he was regarded as one of the top creatives in London, Baz was a difficult senior employee with a recreational drug habit and poor management skills, something both he and Chris had sparred over often. Intersect's clients continued to love Baz Bushell's energy and ideas, so he remained on the plus side of the ledger, but both men knew that the balance of that ledger was constantly under scrutiny.

Chris adopted his captain of the ship posture and tone of voice. "No offense taken, Baz!" he said with a smile. "I hear what you're trying to say."

He continued, addressing everyone: "I know it's an emotive issue. Let's see how it plays out in New York and DC, and then we can discuss it more *if* it goes any further. Maybe the answer will lie in separating the New York and London offices. It could work out that we go in with another agency—and those are my meetings next week—so it may not be our name on the door in any case."

The awkwardness had resettled over the group. The meeting had run over its allotted time, and Laura was desperately trying to silence her pinging phone. "I'm sorry but I need to go," she said.

"OK," said Chris, trying to recover the room and inject some positivity into what had become a difficult conversation. "Let's regroup individually. I know there's a lot on right now, guys, and we're short of resources, but help is on the way, and we are on a *rocket ship*. Let's try to enjoy the ride."

———

Over in Washington DC, in the offices of RBA, Connie and David happened to be discussing the forthcoming opportunity at the National Rifle Association, also with an undercurrent.

"I spoke to Ryan earlier," said David. "He said we are already on the short list, but he's concerned about our lack of advertising experience. Wants to know how we're planning on tackling that. They've been adding some more agency names to their short list."

"He's the fuckin' CEO, for chrissake," said Connie, letting her impatience show and her customary veneer slip. "He can make sure this goes our way. He owes us."

Ryan Perry was indeed the Chief Executive Officer of the NRA and David's longest-standing client. The National Rifle Association had been on the RBA roster since RBA was David

McKenzie Ross and Partners, years before Connie had arrived. David Ross and Ryan Perry had met as law students at Duke University in North Carolina and had remained firm friends ever since. It was also one of the largest and most profitable accounts on the lobbying side of the business at RBA, or anywhere else come to that.

"Well, darling, as I always say, the day you think a client owes you a favor is the day you start looking for another line of work," David said testily.

"You've seen the brief," he continued. "They want to put all their PR, advertising and lobbying into one agency. It's a huge opportunity, and it's also a big risk for us. Ryan was very clear about that—friendship or not—with social media and the threat to their magazine business, they want a single entity that can switch media and money around and understand the business priorities of the organization. And they need better creative ideas— you know that. I think it makes a lot of sense, but you know me—I don't really understand all the digital stuff. I rely on you for that. All I know is that we can't do it on our own."

Connie softened her demeanor. "I know, darlin'. It's just not my favorite idea—partnerin' up with people we don't know. But it sounds like our only option. I'm meetin' this week with John Robins of Universal. You remember? The holdin' company that wants to buy Butterworth Catalogs."

"Of course, I remember," said David. "How's that going?"

"I left Walter Meyer haggling over the details with their lawyers, but I think we're close to a final agreement."

"Did you get the money you wanted? Are you impressed that I haven't asked you how much?"

"Yes, and yes," smiled Connie. "We settled on eight times EBITDA."

David whistled softly. "Well done. He must want you."

The ensuing silence between them had become a more and more frequent barrier between them. It carried the dead weight of all the recently unspoken words and conversations. It papered over the ripe, rich promise of an attractive, wealthy businesswoman in her prime and an increasingly vulnerable man now falteringly late in his career. It covered a growing and uncomfortable divide between their positions and ambitions. And it hinted in its dark edges about the flirtations, affairs and infidelities of the past and the inevitability of those yet to come.

"He's an extremely unattractive man, you know. John Robins. Accountant. Five feet six, max. Halitosis. Really not my type."

"He has money and power."

"Not really power. That's why he needs us. He's a Madison Avenue guy. Doesn't know the difference between George Bush and Georgetown. But he has agencies up the wazoo, and we're in the driver's seat with the sale of my business and this NRA opportunity."

"Well, you take care of him, and I will keep Ryan onsides. I'm sure we will put together an offer that he can't possibly refuse." Davis Ross did his best to sound upbeat as he sat in the soft armchair in Connie's office, surrounded by a hundred silver-framed photos of his flame-haired wife.

"Oh, we will, darlin'. We will."

Later that week, Connie sat in the large utilitarian office of John Robins, CEO of Universal Holdings. She gazed over his shoulder through the weather-stained window looking down at a sweltering Park Avenue scene of yellow taxi cabs and armpit-stained, shirt-sleeved pedestrians sweating their way through the early July humidity of Manhattan. In the corner of the office sat an ice bucket with a half-empty bottle of Dom Perignon. Connie's glass was half full, but untouched for the past ten minutes, as she leaned forward in earnest discussion with Robins.

"Now that we're officially partners, I need your help on this pitch with the NRA," she explained.

"Yes, you mentioned that in your email," said the CEO. "I made some inquiries. We have one agency that was on the long list, but they didn't make the cut. We did find out that they're very high on an agency called Intersect. Do you know them?"

Connie paused. Those guys again, she thought. She said, "They won the US Tourism business last year and set up an office here to manage it, I believe. We still work with the ASTA folks on the public affairs side. They've been impressed with their work. They are not big budgets. And the Intersect CEO is based in London, apparently."

"It's a guy called Chris Crossley who owns and runs the agency. He's American. They're going gangbusters in the UK and beginning to get some traction Stateside," said Robins. "Made their reputation running the Brexit campaign, and now everyone wants a piece of them. It always helps to get a big W. They've taken some accounts from us in the UK and are courting Walmart over here, from what we're hearing. How did they get on NRA's radar?"

"I honestly don't know," said Connie. "Their name has never come up. Same with the tourism folks too. They appeared out of nowhere."

"Well, I've invited him over," said John Robins. "We're going to meet for lunch tomorrow. Do you want to join me?"

"What's your idea?" asked Connie, her mind racing and trying to digest this sudden turn.

"He's obviously got some sort of inside track. I'm not sure we're going to find out what that is, but I'm assuming they will need some sort of help too. Maybe we can all work together on this one. It's certainly big enough, isn't it?"

"David estimates that it's around a $40 million piece of business. And yes, NRA wants all the skills under a single roof. We think they might be lookin' to pull it in-house, or at least a hybrid model—some internal folks plus agencies."

"So, let's see what Mr. Crossley is made of. 1 pm at Michael's?"

———————

Chris glanced at his watch, the Omega Speedmaster Seadiver lying conspicuously but not ostentatiously, he felt, on his athletic wrist. It said what he wanted it to say about his taste—refined, knowing and clasped in a steel bracelet of false modesty. It was nearly time to head uptown for his lunch with John Robins.

The call had come out of the blue a few days previously—the firm voice of an assistant: "Please hold the line for Mr. Robins," followed by the clipped tones of a current titan of Chris's particular industry. Universal Holdings was a collector of companies, a manipulator of marketing services agencies and the fastest-growing, most profitable holding company of its type on the planet. Chris had spoken to a few of his fellow agency CEOs at various conferences and forums over the years. The competing holding companies were most independent agency owners' easiest path to a big payday, the exit that followed the years of toil in creating and growing a privately owned creative enterprise. Robins had a reputation for scooping up the best-in-class agencies in their categories, paying top dollar and then largely leaving them alone if they made their profit targets. However, of late, there seemed to be a trend emerging of smushing some of these smaller companies together to create supergroups for specific categories and in some cases clients.

Chris was intrigued to find out what interest Universal had in Intersect. It was far too early for Chris to contemplate a sale of his business. After all, the agency was growing exponentially now, but it never did any harm to talk and listen; and if Intersect was on the radar of John Robins, then that was its own confirmation of his arrival on a bigger stage.

Chris walked under the dark red awning and past the brass nameplate into the world of the Manhattan power lunch at Michael's of New York. The buzz of conversation floating up from the customers sitting at the circular, white-tableclothed tables rose up to meet him as he approached the maître d's station.

"Mr. Robins's table."

"Certainly sir. This way please."

The maître d led the way across the dining room toward the corner table. As he approached, Chris realized that there were two people already seated there—John Robins, with his unmistakable jowly profile, and the dark red-haired woman whom Chris suddenly remembered from the US Tourism Office last year and whom Emily had noticed at the Four Seasons that same evening. Now, what was her name . . . and why was she here?

They both stood up as Chris approached.

Connie thrust out her hand. "Connie Ross Butterworth. I hope you don't mind me gate-crashin' your lunch," she half-smiled through her Texan drawl.

John Robins, slightly wrongfooted by Connie's initiative, also stretched out his hand. "Chris, it wasn't my intention to surprise you, but I asked Connie to join us as we have a particular subject to discuss. I hope you don't mind?"

Chris did mind. It was a sandbagging. He would never have come to a meeting where he was outnumbered without a pre-agreed agenda and some diligent prep work. He thought this was going to be one-on-one with Robins.

Chris turned his full attention to Connie, his eyes locking with hers, not allowing her to break his gaze. "Of course not," he said. "We haven't formally met before, have we, Connie? I seem to remember seeing you at the US Tourism Office in DC. So great to meet you face to face."

Then, as quickly as he had engaged Connie, he suddenly turned his head away and looked directly at John. "And John, so good to finally meet you. You are just dominating our business right now. Congratulations."

They took their seats, folded their napkins over their laps and looked around the table at each other.

Five minutes later, pleasantries and general market observations having been exchanged, Connie cleared her throat and looked at Chris. "We know you're on the short list for the NRA pitch," she said, "and so, by the way are we. My husband has a thirty-year relationship with them, and more specifically with Ryan Perry, their CEO, whom you may not know."

Chris remained silent. So, this is why, he thought to himself. They need us. And we might need them. Interesting. But I wonder where Universal fits in?

His gaze remained fixed on Connie. That querulous neck, with its plaster-white hue, the blue veins, fine trace work tributaries running below its surface, was fascinating him. Framed by the waves of flame-red hair from the front, she was a Vermeer portrait come to life. And interestingly, the eyes at the center of this seemingly animated porcelain portrait were dead pools. They are almost black, thought Chris. All that movement and color going on around these two limpid, stagnant, fish-like objects, staring out at him with intensity and with nothing going on behind them. If the eyes are the window to the soul, Chris thought to himself, someone should call an undertaker.

"So, Chris," interrupted John Robins, "our approach is to see whether Intersect would be interested in partnering with Universal and RBA for the National Rifle Association opportunity."

"I think I may be missing the part where Universal and RBA fit together," said Chris carefully.

"Of course, we should explain," said Robins. "Earlier this week we acquired Butterworth Catalogs from Connie and her family, and we are excited to have her join Universal as a member of our executive team. We're still figuring out the precise role, aren't we Connie?" he said, glancing across at her. "But the vision for Universal is building cross-discipline teams for clients that deliver best-in-class agency resources without the handicap of having to use just one agency. We think the NRA could be a great chance to test this out and support your bid."

"So, are you expecting that I am interested in selling Intersect?" Chris's voice rose slightly, and he was feeling the beginnings of irritation. Who the hell did this guy and this woman think they were, proposing a joint approach to a pitch with an independent agency that's already on the short list and doing very nicely without them?

Connie jumped in quickly: "Not at all, Chris. Ross Butterworth still remains an independent company outside of Universal. I brought John into the NRA discussion, as we are considerin' partnerin' with an advertising firm for the pitch, and as you know, he owns many." She paused, letting her position sink in.

Then she continued: "I told John how impressed we had been with the work you have done for the US Tourism folks and knowin' that we had heard from Ryan that you were on the consideration list for the Association. We both thought it was worth a conversation with you, as you were in New York, just to, you know, explore . . ."

"So, to be clear," said Chris, "you are suggesting some sort of joint venture between RBA and Intersect for the National Rifle Association business?"

"Seein' if you'd be open to the idea," responded Connie, "and Universal's role is to be as a minority partner in the enterprise—a guarantor of size, scale and resources. We know that's important to the NRA as well as their desire to get the best creative and advocacy advice in the country."

"So, a joint venture between Intersect and RBA with Universal in the background as a show of strength?" Chris was thinking this through as he enunciated it carefully.

"Yes, that's it exactly," said Connie.

"And who would lead the pitch?" asked Chris.

"TBD," said Connie archly, "but I hear you're very good at winnin' new business." The smile was genuine and, Chris was surprised to see, probably her best shot at flirtatious.

"And not to push you," chimed in John Robins, "but I understand the timeline is getting quite tight."

Chris held his tongue. Randy Gardner and the State Department, apparently now in cahoots with the Department of the Treasury, had engineered his agency onto this short list. In the past few days, he had been unable to get much more out of either Randy or the procurement folks at the NRA as to the relative strengths of Intersect's chances—or who Intersect was up against. And he was completely in the dark as to who the Treasury Department's inside source at NRA was and how he or she had enabled Intersect to come to the attention of the NRA and then onto the short list. Someone with some clout, he had to assume.

The US Treasury had someone long term on the inside at the National Rifle Association, and the Intersect bet was just that, a bet. Randy had persuaded them to include Chris because of Intersect's success in London. If Intersect didn't win here, Treasury would just shrug their shoulders and move on, looking for different sources for their nefarious work. He had to assume that they didn't understand the advertising business and weren't to know that $40-million accounts didn't grow on trees, and this one had the potential to become much larger. All Chris could think of as he sat before these circling barracudas was that a win of this size would firmly establish Intersect's reputation within the United States, the biggest advertising market in the world.

As he rapidly made his calculations, Chris remembered his own words to new account managers at the agency: "Over talent and hard work, relationships are the key factor in this business." He'd spent years cultivating his own network in the UK, and in this preliminary estimation, he had the feeling that Connie's husband could possibly be that difference maker as the long-time confidant of Ryan Perry, the NRA CEO.

"Maybe you and I could talk this through in more detail?" said Chris, turning toward Connie and fixing her firmly with what Emily had once described, before the current difficulties of their relationship, as his "McDreamy look."

"I'd be prepared to change my schedule and come to DC tomorrow to meet with the RBA team."

"My, that would be just dandy!" exclaimed Connie. "Although you'll find that the RBA team is pretty much me and David. We'd love to have you join us."

"Excellent. To save some time, I'll get a draft head of agreement together for us to review," said John, appearing back in a conversation that had started to wander away from him.

"That sounds just fine," said Connie.

The setup was complete. Connie and John Robins exchanged brief and satisfied glances as they all continued their lunches.

"Chris, I see you're an Omega man," said John Robins glancing down at Chris's left wrist. "Are you also a Bond fan?"

CHAPTER

TWELVE

"So, the start of the modern NRA can really be traced to what is now called the Cincinnati revolt of 1977." David Ross was holding court in the main meeting room of the RBA offices on 17th Street NW. He had an audience of one: Chris Crossley, who sat upright in a chair pulled up to the vast oval meeting table, his laptop open for taking notes and with a large take-out cup of Starbucks coffee by its side.

Chris jumped in immediately: "That was the year Harlon Carter and Neal Knox came together to lead the Association back to its roots. They were looking for the opportunity to stage a take-over. Some called it a coup, but they saw themselves as the true protectors of the Second Amendment and the saviors of the orig-inal vision of the NRA. They wanted to take power away from the old guard—the existing executives of the organization. They were perceived to be caving in to the political pressure of the day and wanted to move the NRA more toward conservation issues and focus on the sporting use of guns."

Raising his eyebrows, David Ross said, "I see you've done your homework." He went on: "These guys—remember they were the then leadership of the NRA—had quietly done a deal to move the Association headquarters away from DC to the Rocky Mountains to show off their green credentials, if you can believe that? So, the Cincinnati revolt, yes, I think we can say it *was* essentially a coup—brought in the new guard who believed that the NRA had a duty to defend the Second Amendment. They forced the organization to ditch the out-of-touch executives who wanted to return to the days of shooting competitions and hugging trees and rallied the membership to their cause." Davis Ross's voice reflected his passion at the retelling of this story.

"And the NRA is also the oldest association in America, right?" asked Chris.

"One of. Older than the Boy Scouts or Major League baseball," replied David with fervor. "1871."

Chris typed some notes into his computer.

"The NRA became a registered lobby in 1974," continued David. "They hit the ground running and have never looked back."

"When did you become involved, David?" asked Chris, looking up from his screen.

"Around 1985. My law firm was supporting Ryan over the Firearm Owners' Protection Act, and I was assigned to him, as we had been buddies since way back at Duke."

"My dad took his master's at Duke," said Chris.

"Did he now? Smart man. What year?"

"Oh, I can't remember," said Chris. "Probably way before your time."

"Likely not," replied David ruefully, sweeping his white hair back from his forehead.

"Yes, Ryan and I go way back. He was number two in the lobbying wing at that time, and he made his name with the Act. It was a landmark piece of legislation, you know, the Firearm Owners' Protection Act. We authorized mail order sales of guns for the first time, kept lists of gunowners away from the government. That's why there is no national gun registry and never will be."

David paused for breath in a brief moment of wistful silence. Then he continued, "So, Ryan encouraged me to set up my own lobbying firm shortly after that. I've had him as a client ever since. I've been very blessed."

"What do you think he's really looking for with this marketing agency search?" asked Chris.

"Honestly, knowing Ryan, I think he's looking for more control," responded David hesitantly. "I know he gets frustrated with his team not speaking with one voice. The PR folks, the advertising folks, the publishing operation, the designers, us. He really wants it under one roof. And I think he has a vision for the NRA that is broader than being seen as a defender of the Second Amendment. He wants the NRA to be a defender of *all* this country's freedoms, and also serve as a model for other democracies. I don't think I'm overstating that. They've had eight years of playing defense under Obama; now with Trump he knows they have a staunch ally and an advocate. That's huge. Of course, the irony of all that is that gun sales are likely to go down."

"How's that?" Chris looked puzzled.

"The fear of gun restrictions drove sales under Obama," said David. "You know when there's a hurricane coming, and all the bread leaves the shelves of the supermarket? Same with gun sales in 2008. Folks thought he was coming for their weapons, so they stocked up. The gun manufacturers have had the best eight years of sales in their history."

"How many guns did they sell?" asked Chris, furiously typing notes into his laptop.

"Hard to say; they don't broadcast their numbers. Overall, it's safe to say that we're probably approaching 500 million civilian-owned firearms by now."

"Phew!"

David Ross grinned. "It's a big number, isn't it? And there are only 6 million registered firearms in the whole country."

"There are half a billion guns and only 6 million registered?" Chris was incredulous.

"We did that," said David Ross proudly.

The door to the conference room opened, and Connie walked in.

"What did I miss?" she asked.

"David was giving me the lay of the land," replied Chris. "I'm trying to figure out how we can make them look better. You guys have already set such a high bar."

"That's why you're here," said Connie, flashing a smile at Chris. "We can't wait to see the advertising guru in action!"

"By the way," she added, "where are your bags? I didn't see them in reception."

"Oh, I dropped my overnight bag at the hotel," said Chris. "I'll check in a little later."

"Nonsense. We won't hear of it, will we darlin'? You're stayin' with us tonight, I insist. We have a guest room all ready for you."

"That's very kind of you, but I have all sorts of work to do and calls to make," said Chris. "I don't want to disturb you."

"Not at all," said Connie firmly. "Nuestra casa es su casa. You'll have a desk and internet in your room. You are our guest; it's as simple as that. Now let's get to work on this presentation."

Later that evening, after a long day interacting with the Ross Butterworths, Chris sat at the narrow desk in the large guest room in the Georgetown mansion with his computer screen throwing its ghostly light on his nowadays nearly famous, currently very weary, features. It had been exhausting being caught in the middle of one very aggressive and one very defensive component of a married couple. Not that they had dissimilar ideas about how to approach the task; it was that each of them insisted that a particular point, or phrase or visual or strategic approach should be executed exactly as they envisaged it. And Chris, while self-awareness and holding his tongue weren't exactly his strong suits either, was thrust into the unfamiliar role of referee and scribe as the outline of their presentation came together through the afternoon.

He had tried to get out of the office to call Randy Gardner at the State Department in London. He needed to let him know that Intersect wouldn't be pitching the NRA business alone. He wanted Randy to let whoever was on the inside at the Association know that RBA and Intersect were now one entity in the contest and ask if they were able to start tipping the scales toward their bid. But by the time the opportunity arose to break away from the family feud that the meeting had become, it was too late in London for him to reasonably bother Randy. The same with the Intersect London office—so now he was busy scrolling through the raft of emails and text messages that had been unleashed into his inboxes during the London day.

The good news from the UK was that hiring was picking up and clients were, it seemed, currently happy, or least not unhappy, with the levels of service and creative work. He had received a couple of dry messages from Dai Davies—short and to the point, as he would have expected from him. There was nothing from Emily Upchurch; she was obviously making her own statement to him now that he had told everyone that Dai was in charge in his absence. Chris normally relied on Emily's daily updates for color, context and insight. He sent Dai a note asking him to forward Emily's emails directly to him in the future. Chris was not someone to suffer from a guilty conscience, but he knew he needed to spend some time making repairs with Emily and made a mental note to move it up to the top of his to-do list when he got back to the UK.

Chris was also considering who would accompany him from the Intersect New York office as the potential account person for the NRA when the pitch meeting took place in Fairfax in a couple of weeks' time. He'd spent some hours with the account director that Emily had hired to manage the US Tourism business over the previous couple of days, Rebecca Taylor. Rebecca was smart, personable and attractive. She was also, as flagged by the London team, very young. He couldn't lay his hands on her résumé in his files, but he remembered that as he left for DC yesterday, she had mentioned that she had been to college at Georgetown University, so that might be a hometown advantage to pull out. He'd overheard one of the creatives refer to her as "foxy"—an expression he hadn't heard in a long while, and he remembered thinking how appropriate a description it was for her at the same time as he was considering the inappropriateness of the remark.

Chris pushed back his chair from the desk. It was close to 11 pm, he still hadn't changed from his work clothes or had a shower, and he was beginning to fade. His mind wandered to the night before he left London for New York and his second date with Emily Smith, the executive from the National Lottery. All of the ice had been broken that evening and seemingly all her reservations and reserve about moving on from her estranged husband too. They'd discovered that they had a real connection to each other and a common desire to enjoy each other's company without any need for discussion or introspection. Chris had jumped in a 6 am Uber back to his place to collect his bags and a fresh set of clothes to head out to the Manhattan office the following morning. While he had thought a lot about that night, he'd been wrapped up in work ever since and not been in touch with her since he'd arrived in the States.

Chris impulsively picked up his phone. He owed Ms. Emily Smith a check-in, and he smiled to himself as his fingers hovered over the phone keyboard. He typed a couple of suggestive and cryptic remarks, added an eggplant emoji and hit send with an expansive gesture and a grin; then he lifted himself from the desk to get ready for bed. Suddenly there was a soft knock on his bedroom door, and it opened slowly to reveal Connie Ross Butterworth, dressed in a bathrobe.

"Just checkin' that everything is all right? I saw your light on. David went to bed."

Connie stood framed in the doorway, her copper hair cascading around each side of her long neck, the robe very slightly off one of her shoulders.

Chris shifted uncomfortably, caught mid-stride toward the bathroom, phone in hand.

"Everything is fine. Thank you, Connie. Appreciate it."

"Well just let me know if there is anythin' I can do for you. It's a pleasure to have you here."

She stood expectantly in the doorway.

"It's all good," said Chris. "I'll see you in the morning first thing. I need to get back to New York in the afternoon."

"Goodnight, Chris."

"Goodnight, Connie."

Next morning Chris rolled over to silence his 6 am alarm call. The locked phone screen showed a blizzard of messages awaiting his attention.

The one all in caps from Emily Upchurch caught his immediate attention: "WTF?"

Chris's heart sank. He realized immediately. *Shit*, he'd sent his text last night to the wrong Emily! Talk about pouring gasoline onto a smoldering fire! He quickly dialed her number.

"What?"

"Em, I'm really sorry. I sent that text last night to you by mistake."

"Oh for God's sake, Chris—who are you fucking kidding?"

"No, really. I've been seeing Emily Smith. You know, the CMO at National Lottery. It wasn't meant for you. I apologize."

There was a silence.

"And this makes me feel better how?" Emily sounded choked up. "You ignore me for a year after DC, send me an explicit text and then tell me it was meant for another Emily. Gee thanks, Chris. You're a real stud."

The line went dead.

Chris scrolled through the other texts and emails quickly. An email from Dai Davies told him that Emily had been to see him very upset and was considering filing a complaint—could Chris please fill him in.

A message from Randy Gardner merely said enigmatically, "Good Luck!"

Chris quickly showered, and as he did, he sorted through his priorities and calculated how to lessen the damage with Emily Upchurch. He'd made a mistake last summer, and his way of dealing with it had been to ignore it. It wasn't his style to explain himself, he said to himself; she must know that it was a one-off, but he also needed to demonstrate how important she was to the business without leading her on with any behavior that might be misinterpreted.

He came down the enormous staircase of the Ross Butterworth mansion and turned into the kitchen. Connie was sitting on one side of the breakfast counter with a bright green smoothie in front of her, with David sitting on the other side of the counter with a cup of coffee, his head buried in the *Wall Street Journal*.

"Good mornin', Chris," said Connie brightly. "What can I get you? Eggs?"

"Just coffee, thanks."

"Good man," said David.

"We've just had confirmation of a meetin' with Ryan Perry at NRA at 10 am, so we're goin' to need to make a move before the traffic gets too bad." Connie was sucking up her drink concoction, leaving a bright red band of lipstick on the white paper straw.

"I didn't know that was in the cards," replied Chris carefully, not showing his irritation.

These two were a piece of work. This was the first he'd heard of a meeting, and they had obviously sprung it to wrong-foot him.

"We thought it would be a great idea to let him know about our partnership in person and let him meet you," David chimed in. "He's found half an hour in his calendar for us. We thought you'd appreciate it," he deadpanned.

"Of course," replied Chris. "What about our meeting with John Robins?" he asked, looking at Connie.

"I pushed us back to one o'clock," said Connie.

"Fine, I just need to make a couple of quick calls." Chris picked up the coffee that Connie had just poured for him and headed back upstairs.

"The car service will be here at 8:30," Connie called after him.

———

The NRA head office in Fairfax, Virginia, was a smoked glass–fronted, ten-story 1990s' eyesore of an office building sitting practically astride the roaring traffic of Route 66 and looking for all the world like every other suburban corporate HQ in the area.

The dynamic had shifted on the car ride to Fairfax. David, seated in the front, spelled out to Chris his expectations for the meeting.

"He'll want to know about the strength of your team here in the US and your experience with running an account like this. We only have a short time, so keep it high level. Oh, and I assume you're a gun owner? Let him know what you have. And a few compliments will go a long way. Sorry to be telling you what you already know. What's that great British expression? I'm teaching my grandmother how to suck eggs? Remember, I know Ryan well. Oh, and he's a golf nut."

Chris kept quiet, as David didn't appear to be wanting answers. The golf nugget would be an easy in. The gun ownership slightly less so. The truth was that he'd lived in the UK for the greater part of the previous fifteen years. There was no gun culture there at all; in fact, the opposite viewpoint prevailed. Acquiring a gun was an onerous process, and handguns were virtually banned in any case. He had no need for a rifle in south London, and he reflected, he hadn't really thought about guns for a long time. He remembered from his childhood that they thought his father probably had one in a safe, although no one had ever seen it. In the US you assumed most people owned at least one gun, and in the UK you most certainly assumed the opposite. When the NRA had come up in the conversation with Randy Gardner a few short weeks ago, Chris had assumed he was benignly neutral about guns and, being American, fundamentally in favor of the Second Amendment. As the business opportunity began hurtling into the foreground, he was beginning to realize that he was holding some misgivings. The more he had heard from David the previous day, the more he realized that he would be stepping into a fervid, even fanatical environment. There was no place for snowflake neutrality here; he would need to demonstrate a passionate embrace of the NRA's mission, and as he listened to David Ross, it seemed that merely talking the talk would not be sufficient.

As they approached the NRA head office from the freeway exit, he needed to ask himself some hard questions. How hard can it be? he thought. If I can be a Brexiteer, I can totally be a gun nut.

Ryan Perry was clearly a man used to getting his own way.

The CEO of arguably the most powerful lobby in the country was medium height, fit, tanned and immaculately dressed in a dark blue suit and red tie. He spoke confidently and authoritatively in response to Chris's question, "What does success look like for you in this process?"

"Great ideas, great execution and great people," he said firmly. "We need a team we can trust, and we need to reduce some overhead and replace some dead wood here."

"David knows this. I'm pleased y'all have decided to join forces," said Connie.

There was a lot of constrained energy behind those gleaming eyes, Chris thought to himself as he sized up Perry. Perry was an animated man, his hands moving constantly, his eyes darting around the room. His assistant had joined him in the meeting, her old-fashioned notepad open, furiously taking notes in pencil.

"Now that we have a friendly administration," Ryan Perry continued, "it's time for us to take some major initiatives."

"And what form will they take?" Chris immediately asked.

Perry paused, cocked his head slightly and, in what Chris was beginning to notice as a nasal whine, replied with a dismissive gesture and tone of voice, "Young man, if you end up working with us, you'll be given those orders on day one."

Ryan Perry shifted his gaze to David Ross: "David, has your whole team signed the NDA?"

"Yes, we have dropped off all the paperwork with Pam," replied David quickly.

"Good. Any other questions? I need to get on with my day."

"Well, it's been a great honor to meet you, sir," said Chris. "We look forward to presenting our ideas in a couple of weeks, and thank you for the opportunity."

Perry relaxed his set jaw momentarily and extended his hand to Chris.

"And will we be in this meeting room, sir?" asked Chris as he shook Ryan Perry's hand vigorously.

Taken aback at such a mundane question, Ryan Perry looked confused. "Um, well yes, I suppose so. This is our main conference area," he replied.

"Thank you, sir. I like to be well prepared," replied Chris briskly. "Thanks again for your time."

Ryan Perry left the room; his assistant remained.

Chris moved over to the large window overlooking the long lines of traffic crawling in both directions along Route 66. He motioned to David and Connie to join him.

He pointed to the exit junction adjacent to the building in which they stood:

"Can we find out who owns those billboards?" he asked, pointing to two enormous roadside advertisements, one for car insurance and one for McDonald's.

"It's going to cost a lot of money to get them to turn them over to us for a couple of days," said Connie, immediately realizing what Chris had in mind.

"It may be worth it," said Chris.

Davis Ross nodded approvingly.

Chris and Connie were running behind for the meeting with John Robins at the Trump National Hotel on Pennsylvania Avenue. They dropped David off at the RBA offices and headed over to meet their erstwhile partner. Chris was mulling over the fast pace of recent events as they walked into the opulent lobby area of the former post office building. Robins was seated on a couch, and they grabbed a couple of seats to join him.

"How's it going?" the rumpled and pint-sized CEO asked.

"It's comin' together very nicely," responded Connie quickly. "Chris has been invaluable, and we had a helpful meetin' with Ryan Perry this mornin'."

"Which is why we're runnin' a little late," she added.

"Good to hear," said Robins. "What can I do to help?"

"Well, for a start, we need to secure two billboard sites next to their offices for the pitch," said Connie.

"I'm sure we can arrange that," said Robins. "We're the biggest buyer of outdoor advertising in the country, so someone will be owing us that favor."

"I'm going to need a production house for a fast turnaround for the ads themselves," said Chris, running through his mental checklist.

"Just let my office know what you need," said Robins. "We're here to support our partners. Speaking of, I have a draft of the joint venture agreement for each of your agencies to review." He handed manila envelopes to each of them.

"Chris, I've taken the liberty of including a separate proposal for you to consider. I hope you don't mind. I would like you to offer Universal the first option to acquire Intersect if you decide to sell the business within the next five years. I've included some ranges of multiples to show you how serious we are and how much we admire your agency."

Chris smiled tightly. "Thank you, John. We don't intend to sell Intersect anytime soon but really appreciate your interest."

"Of course," said Robins. "Let's get this pitch won and start working together; who knows what the future may bring. I just wanted to put a marker down. I'm a big fan of your work."

Chris slipped the envelope into his briefcase and glanced over toward Connie. "I really need to make a move," he said. "We have more work to do on the proposal before I head back to New York."

"You go ahead and get with David; he's leadin' this for us," replied Connie. "I have a few things I need to discuss with John. Hopefully I will see you before you leave."

Chris got up, shook hands with John Robins and nodded toward Connie. Her titian locks flowed around her pale, small features. But what struck him most was the faint, reptilian glitter in her coal black eyes as she returned his gaze.

CHAPTER
THIRTEEN

Chris was in front of his laptop in Intersect's Union Square office talking via video conference with Dai Davies.

"I sent the offer and the JV paperwork to the lawyers," said Dai. "I went through them both first, as you asked."

"And?" asked Chris.

"Well, the offer to acquire us could definitely be very lucrative."

"We're not selling," said Chris firmly.

"I know, but if you start building that US office the way you built this one, you might find it very tempting, one day soon," Dai said as he smiled over the video conference screen.

"OK, let me know when you hear back from the lawyers on the joint venture agreement," said Chris. "That one is urgent."

"It looked pretty standard. Are you sure you want to go this route?"

"Honestly, no," said Chris, "but now that I've met David Ross, who by the way is way less scary than his wife, I don't think we have a choice. He's good buddies with Ryan Perry—they go way back."

"Then why do they need us?" asked Dai.

"Perry knows they don't have advertising expertise, and he wants a big campaign. Also, I think us winning the US Tourism business from under RBA's noses made some waves in that lobbying world. Plus, we were on the short list already."

"One day you're going to tell me how that happened," said Dai with a smile. "The only clause that stood out in the JV to me was the elaborate non-disparagement clause. Did you see it? If one of the partners wants out after a year, each has the ability to buy the departing party out at a pre-agreed price, but there's also a sentence in there that if one of the parties brings disrepute on the partnership, then the others can dissolve the agreement. I've asked the lawyers to give us a view on that."

"Well, given Universal has hundreds of agencies and more than a few dodgy clients, that might be useful for us," grinned Chris. "What else is going on?"

"You've really pissed off Emily, mate."

"Oh, I know. That was my bad. I sent her a text message meant for someone else, and she didn't take it well."

"I mean this as a friend, Chris. You really need to keep it in your pants as far as the workplace is concerned. She wanted to file a complaint."

"Noted, Dai. What else?"

"I think it's all OK. Baz has been shooting his mouth off a bit about the volume of work, but nothing new there."

"Yeah, I was going to get him to oversee the NRA ideas, but he's not keen."

"None of us are, Chris. You know that. Guns are not fun."

"I get it. But it's a different vibe in the US. Let everyone know that we're in a joint venture and our name won't be on the door. I can't walk away from a $40 million opportunity that's being handed to us on a plate."

"Alright, mate. Good luck."

Dai signed off, and Chris stared at the blank screen. He knew that the adrenaline of the chase for the National Rifle Association business was potentially clouding his judgment, but the raw facts were on his side, he reasoned. Guns were part of the culture here; the Brits simply didn't get that. The joint venture gave Intersect some cover in case of adverse publicity. And while he would prefer not to share the $40 million in billings, the partnership with RBA—and, in particular he now saw, Universal—put his agency in a strong position for future collaborations. Plus, having a possible exit sale to Universal if and when he decided to sell the business was a warm feeling not to be ignored.

The State Department referral from Randy Gardner in the first place continued to nag at him, though. Who was the Treasury Department insider at NRA who had got Intersect on the short list? No one obvious had surfaced in any of the discovery calls that he'd been on with the different functions within the Association. He must ask Rebecca if he'd missed any critical meetings. And thinking of her, she had really risen to the occasion in his estimation during this process. She was very smart, asked great questions, took insightful notes and was super organized. He needed to thank Emily for the hire, and that would also give him the chance to try and smooth things over between the two of them.

He picked up his phone and got Emily's voicemail.

"You've reached the voicemail of Emily Upchurch. Please leave a message."

"Em, just wanted to let you know that Rebecca is working out real well on the NRA pitch and to thank you for another great hire. Also, to apologize again for the text mix-up. Hope you don't hate me. Let's chat soon. Bye."

Keeping his phone in hand, he dialed Randy Gardner at the State Department and got through to his assistant.

"Hi Moneypenny, is he there?"

A giggle came from the other end. "He's between meetings. Let me try for you, Chris."

A pause, then, "Chris—I'm rushing around. What can I do for you?" Randy's cheery tone transcended the 3,000 miles to Union Square.

"Just checking in, Randy. We seem in a good position to win this NRA thing. Obviously, we have to produce some great ideas and do an amazing presentation. Curious as to the next steps with you guys. Will you and I continue to work together if it lands?"

"It's outside our jurisdiction, Chris. I'll need to introduce you to my Treasury counterpart in DC when the time comes. Hang tight. I'm sure you've got this, Chris."

"No problem, Randy. Before you go, and you may not be able to answer, but can you tell me their inside guy at NRA? There's no obvious candidate we've come across yet."

There was a slight pause and then, "I'm surprised at you, Chris Crossley." There was a chuckle from Randy. "You've been working with him."

Chris's mind momentarily went blank, and then it hit him like a punch in the solar plexus. "David Ross?"

"Give that man a cigar!"

"Now it makes sense."

"Apparently, he wants out—the Treasury had him on some tax issues, and he's been cooperating for the last decade. They gave him the option of recruiting a replacement, and they had your name from me. He's apparently very impressed with you, by the way."

Chris felt sick. He was being played. Played by the government and played by the Ross Butterworths. Or was it merely David Ross? He'd agreed to share the Brexit information with the State Department out of a sense of patriotism and, if he was honest, a sense of managed excitement and danger. Being a spy was on every schoolboy's wish list, wasn't it? And the quid pro quo from the government with the introduction of the US Tourism business was his on-ramp to building Intersect's presence in his home country. It had been so far so good at that point; now he was staring at some unfolding consequences of continuing with that journey.

Much later in the day, Chris had made peace with the situation. He reasoned that his alarm had been the result of not being in possession of all the facts—and not fully thinking things through. Think about the opportunity, he said to himself. The bottom line was the bottom line, a credo he kept close to his heart and often repeated to others. He had created the opportunity to significantly grow his US business. The National Rifle Association was a massive financial and strategic opportunity for Intersect. He was bothered by the RBA complication; for sure, he had failed to read David Ross completely. And he didn't trust Connie one iota. But from a business outcome point of view, he couldn't see much downside. David Ross clearly knew about Intersect's government connections, and now it was up to Chris to show David Ross that his own motivation was purely patriotic, not as a result of some transgression or payback owed to the Department of the Treasury. He would need to have an open conversation with RBA and the Treasury contact—he couldn't afford to be "outed" at some future point if David Ross was wriggling off his self-made hook. There would have to be a confidentiality agreement—an "omerta," as the Mafia dons would have it—a vow of silence.

As he was thinking everything through, there was a soft knock at his office door.

"Hello, Boss—you ready for a catch-up?" The pleasing features of Rebecca Taylor appeared framed in the doorway. With her blonde hair falling neatly at shoulder length around her attractive face and perfect white teeth, she had the look of an idealized account executive conjured up by central casting if central casting had been lazily assessing its top two choices that day. Rebecca had a presence, as well as the looks, and was very aware of the effect that she had on those around her, particularly those of the male persuasion.

What a very self-composed young woman, Chris thought to himself, covertly admiring her figure silhouetted in the doorway, as he answered her. "Come on in Rebecca. What's new?"

"You said six o' clock, right?"

"Absolutely. Oh Lord, it's nearly 6:30! I'm sorry to keep you waiting."

"No worries. I could see you were busy."

"We could always do the catch-up over a drink if you are free," Chris ventured.

"Oh, sure . . . that would be great. I'm mean to be seeing someone for dinner later, but we can go through everything out of the office, definitely." She stammered slightly in getting the words out.

"Great!" said Chris. "We'll go to The NoMad around the corner. Give me five minutes."

On home turf, as he now liked to think of The NoMad Hotel, Chris relaxed, nursing a gin and tonic in the privacy of the members bar, with Rebecca sitting alongside him, her laptop out, and going through her notes of the day's meetings to relay to Chris. Her long hair fell forward over her face as she read, and he noticed the discrete tattoo of a peace sign on the inside of her right wrist as her fingers brushed gracefully over the keyboard. They walked through the upcoming pitch with the NRA, checking through progress on the creative and the presentation itself, confirming dates and logistics. Rebecca, having been slightly surprised by the off-the-cuff invitation, was now composed and comfortable as she responded easily to Chris's questions and comments. They completed the NRA checklist and paused.

"Great, thank you," said Chris. "It feels like we're in a good place."

"So, do you actually stay here all the time?" asked Rebecca, interested, and changing the subject.

"Yes, I don't have an apartment in the city," said Chris. "My permanent home is still in London. I did a deal with these guys for a regular room for the next couple of months. As you can see, it's not too shabby and pretty easy for the office." He grinned and held her gaze, aware of the effect that he would be creating. Rebecca blushed slightly and smiled.

"So, where is home for you, Rebecca?"

"I live in Brooklyn with a friend from college. My family's from Old Greenwich, Connecticut."

"No way! I grew up in New Canaan!" exclaimed Chris. "What a small world."

A half hour and another drink later, Chris and Rebecca had moved their barstools slightly closer together, as they exchanged conversation about places they held in common, including junior and grade schools, churches and country clubs. Their families had inhabited much of the same privileged lives and upbringing, albeit that their respective childhoods were separated by a decade or more.

"How often do you go back to New Canaan?" asked Rebecca.

"I don't," replied Chris. "It's complicated. I stay here in the city, work hard, work out and do my own thing."

"Same," replied Rebecca. Her look to Chris was direct and uncomplicated.

"Then you need to get some hobbies," laughed Chris, turning his face more closely toward hers.

Rebecca, animated after two glasses of wine, leaned forward toward him, her fingers brushing his hand:

"Oh, I have hobbies," she breathed. "How are the rooms here?" she asked, looking up at him, frankly and guilelessly.

As Chris, whose stomach had suddenly knotted with thick desire, was about to respond, his phone, laying between them on the bar, pinged with an incoming text message.

They both glanced down at the screen at the same time to see the name Connie Ross Butterworth materialize and then disappear.

"She gets everywhere," Rebecca said immediately, smiling.

Chris also smiled, then paused. And then suddenly alert, he asked, "Have you been talking to her much about the pitch?"

"Oh no, not at all," said Rebecca. "Just based on my prior experience with her."

Chris continued to show confusion. "How so?"

"You know, when I interned there after college," Rebecca replied. "She's a very accomplished lady, but very demanding, shall we say?"

Chris was having difficulty processing this latest piece of information. "Say again?" he asked. "You interned at RBA?"

"Yes, of course. I thought that's why you hired me. Emily told me because I already knew the US Tourism client, you guys were prepared to offer me a more senior position."

"Oh yes, absolutely. It had slipped my mind." It was Chris's turn to stammer slightly. "You've been doing such an amazing job, Rebecca, I'd entirely forgotten. I'd figured we had trained you completely ourselves." Chris leaned away slightly, as his eyes masked and he let his teeth smile at Rebecca.

There was a momentary and awkward silence.

"Where is your dinner?" Chris asked.

Rebecca realized that the moment before the text message had gone forever. She looked down and gathered up her purse from the stool beside her.

"Meatpacking District," she said. "I should order an Uber and get going."

Chris walked Rebecca through the hotel to the lobby entrance to wait for her ride. He'd struggled to compose himself and was boiling with anger at his own weakness and lack of attention to detail. He wondered how much information had been flowing to RBA from his office. How could he have missed the internship information? He pieced it back together in his mind—of course Georgetown University; of course Emily would have looked for someone who had some knowledge of the US Tourism client; and yes, he'd probably glanced over her résumé when Emily hired her, but he hadn't digested what was obviously an extremely brief work experience section of her young life so far.

The whole day had been a series of unwelcome revelations—David Ross had turned out to be the NRA mole; Emily Upchurch was so upset with him, he had now broken their almost subliminal work bond; and now the girl he had entrusted to help him win the NRA account had turned out to be a potential plant by a woman who was beginning to look more and more like a threat, not a partner.

Chris ordered another drink at the bar and took it up to his room, alone.

———————

"Did you see that note from Chris Crossley?" Connie barked, walking into David's office.

"Which one of the many?"

"The one about the photo shoot."

"Ha! I quite liked that one," laughed David. "I think Ryan will appreciate it too."

"It's ridiculous. I'm not posin' in a dress carrying an AR-15. I've never heard of anythin' so stupid in my life." Connie's voice was close to a shriek.

"I don't think they specified the type of gun, Connie. The idea is to show the NRA their new team packing heat. And plastered all over that giant billboard outside their offices. Ryan will love it."

"These advertising people are the worst. They're so tacky."

"Maybe so," conceded David, "but I like the energy, don't you? We're not going to lose it for the lack of creativity. What did you think about the campaign ideas?"

"They're OK," conceded Connie. "I don't think we're goin' to blow them away."

David smiled at the phrasing. Connie was blissfully unaware of the double entendre.

"Well young Mr. Crossley and his account manager are on their way by all accounts," said David. "We're meeting them at the photographer's studio."

"Oh Lord, he's bringin' Rebecca, is he?"

"Who's Rebecca?"

"David Ross, you never stopped gawkin' at her the whole time she interned for us. I know you haven't forgotten her."

David kept his counsel.

"He'll probably have her pose in a bikini," sniped Connie. "Now *that* will certainly make your day."

Chris had felt awkward at first. He hadn't held a gun since high school, and carrying the semiautomatic rifle, albeit knowing that it wasn't loaded, had made him feel slightly nervous. But as the beat of "Born in the USA" and the familiarity of being in front of the camera started to work on him, he quickly forgot that he was carrying a weapon and got into the session. He'd chosen a more American cut for his gray charcoal Brioni suit, and the addition of the aviator shades was a perfect touch. James Bond meets Reservoir Dogs, the photographer had shouted out at him over the constant and pounding soundtrack.

David Ross also looked like a natural—who wouldn't be comforted knowing that this white-haired patrician with the strong jawline and steely blue eyes was there to protect them? David stood resolutely, as if in front of his beleaguered farmstead, fighting off raiders, staring them down and holding his classic Wyatt Earp double-barreled shotgun as the ultimate but inevitable last resort.

Rebecca simply looked stunning—the long legs, the flowing blonde hair, the sleeveless and daring sheer blouse and in her hand, the blunt dangerous-looking copper-colored Glock pistol were the stuff of fantasies. *Charlie's Angels* called out the photographer, but in truth the projection was more Lara Croft than Farrah Fawcett and then probably more Lara Croft's renegade, drug-running niece in a franchise extension that had yet to be dreamed up by Hollywood.

Connie was the problem. She didn't want to be there, and it showed. She looked over all the weapons that the NRA publicity and safety people had brought and shook her head.

"This isn't goin' to work for me," she said.

Chris raised his eyebrows toward David, who shrugged.

In the end, the photographer brought in a high stool, and Connie sat with her hands clasped around a box of ammo on her lap.

"That's the best you're going to get," whispered David to Chris as they passed by close to each other.

Rebecca kept her distance from both Chris and Connie and flirted shamelessly with David, who was all in—immediately and momentarily reliving his younger self while he too kept his distance from Connie.

As the session came toward a close, the photographer brought them all together for a group shot. But the chemistry clearly wasn't there—the energy had left the studio—so he separated Chris and said in a low voice: "I'll need to do a composite for the team shot. Don't worry, it will look great. I got some good stuff."

Chris nodded and said: "Thanks for making it happen. Appreciate your passion."

"No problem. Best of luck with the pitch."

CHAPTER
FOURTEEN

Chris was on his feet in the warm, full meeting room. The presentation was in full swing; the mostly male faces around the table were all directed to the front of the room where an animated Chris stood to one side of the screen pointing at the bold lettering on the slide being projected for all to read along:

MAGAZINE HALF-EMPTY
US private citizens already own 45% of the world's guns.

MAGAZINE HALF-FULL
Only 3 in 10 Americans currently own a gun.

"So, the *glass* could be seen as half-empty." Chris emphasized the word "glass" before adding, "Or in our case, the *magazine* might be seen as half-empty. . . ." He paused a couple of beats to let the small joke land, which it did. "You've done such a great job in this country that we already own nearly half of the world's guns."

"But does that mean we are running out of growth?" He posed the question looking around the room, imploring his audience to deeply consider the question before jumping in to answer it himself in his most commanding and compelling tone of voice.

He continued: "Let's instead think of that *magazine* . . ."—again a small pause to let the word "magazine" settle—"as half-full. We have plenty of ammunition left."

Chris paused, and then with a smile he said: "Only 30% of Americans actually own a gun. Let that sink in"—again the pause, the crisp and precise enunciation and delivery and the look around the room.

Chris's gaze fell on each audience member individually, before he continued: "So we believe that there is a lot of runway for the National Rifle Association to grow gun ownership in this country. To strengthen its position as the single greatest defender of this country's freedoms."

There was a pause in the room, and Chris had control.

"Providing . . . ," again a pause.

"Providing that we can *continue* to show the country . . . and the *world* . . ."

Another pause in delivery, and Chris gazed fervently out into his audience as he brought his message home: "that the right to bear arms is necessary to the *security* of a free State."

Ryan Perry glanced around the table at his team to see if these words had had the same impact on them as they had clearly had on him. He need not have been concerned. There was a vigorous nodding of heads and a generosity of body language leaning toward Chris as the NRA heads of marketing and communications, as well as Ryan Perry's second in command, Bob Cotton, creased matching smiles.

David Ross felt ecstatic. This was what he had been hoping for as they had crossed the parking lot earlier that morning and he had laid his hand on Chris Crossley's shoulder. "Knock it out of the park," he had murmured.

"You know that we will," Chris had replied.

David glanced across at his wife, who had been sitting erect and without expression for most of the morning. The final rehearsals for the presentation in the RBA offices had been filled with tension over the previous two days. As they ran through the strategy, the draft slides and the campaign ideas, Connie's role in the meeting had gradually been reduced. Over the previous twenty-plus years, David had been the face of the RBA relationship with the NRA as Ryan Perry's close confidant and the long-term lobbyist on the account. Connie's role, after she married David, joined the firm and started to propel RBA's growth in other areas, had always been a secondary one with their client in Fairfax (as they liked to describe the organization), and as the response to the new opportunity coalesced, it appeared that it would remain that way. David was enthused with the energy and ideas that Intersect was bringing to the table, and he and Chris had formed a formidable double act as they toiled for long hours in the RBA offices, consuming coffee, sandwiches and Diet Cokes in search of the perfect combination of insights, ideas and theater.

Chris, meanwhile, was reaching the climax of his morning's adrenaline-fueled performance.

The slide on the screen did a slow dissolve, and a new one appeared, displaying the words:

MONARCHY

OLIGARCHY

AUTHORITARIAN

TOTALITARIAN

COMMUNIST

All appeared in bold black type and then disappeared, one by one.

They were replaced by one word, outlined in black and colored in bands of red, white and blue, appearing from the bottom and filling the screen:

DEMOCRACY

"For 250 years," Chris said, "America has redefined the concept of a truly free people." His voice, benefiting from an accent slightly softened by fifteen years of transatlantic influence, and carrying an authority granted normally only to Hollywood voice-over talent, was reaching to the back of the crowded room.

The word "DEMOCRACY" on the screen suddenly morphed into another:

FREEDOM

"After freedom of speech," Chris said, "our forefathers and the architects of the world's greatest democracy gave us the *next* great freedom. The right to bear arms."

Chris had entered full evangelical mode. He stood at the front of the room, unconstrained by notes, and he projected charisma and fervor toward the seated group.

The image on the screen changed behind him, and a montage of figures appeared, one by one and dissolved.

General Patton, John Wayne, Davy Crockett, Daniel Boone and Annie Oakley flashed by in quick succession. Then at faster pace, the screen showed Nelson Mandela, Gandhi, Mel Gibson as William Wallace in *Braveheart*, Bruce Willis in *Die Hard*, Clint Eastwood in *Magnum Force* and then stopped on the famous painting of Paul Revere on horseback.

Chris moved a step closer to his audience: "Our enemies," he said, "may try to take our lives, but they will never take. . . ," at this point the screen reverted to two words:

OUR FREEDOM

Unnoticed by the people around the table, Rebecca Taylor had moved to the window, and with a dramatic flourish, she pulled hard on the cord that drew the blinds to let in a flood of sunlight.

"We invite you to view your next campaign," said Chris. "Please go to the window." He was looking directly at Ryan Perry.

Ryan Perry, with a surprised look on his face, rose from his chair and walked the few steps to the large window that overlooked Route 66. Others followed.

Facing them were the two giant billboards that guarded Exit 57, normally given over to fast food and insurance ads.

One had the word "FREEDOM" stretched across the top of the advertisement. Underneath was the iconic image of George Washington crossing the Delaware River, and below, in the bottom right, the three letters NRA.

The other billboard was a two-story-high, black-and-white photograph of four of the people currently in the room gazing back at the room from across the freeway. In this image, Chris stood cradling an AR-15, his strong-jawed, handsome face impassive behind a pair of Rayban Aviator sunglasses. Next to him David Ross held a shotgun across his body, the last defender of the American frontier, seemingly staring into the room from the intersection. Rebecca Taylor, a blonde avenging angel with her Glock pistol nonchalantly in hand, was, truthfully, a traffic hazard to the distracted drivers below. And finally, Connie Ross Butterworth imperiously gazing outward, a box of ammunition in her seated lap, for all the world the somewhat sinister armorer for this group, who were described simply at the bottom of the billboard:

YOUR TEAM

Chris cleared his throat, and the gaggle of people clustered around the window broke their gazes to look back into the room.

"And that, ladies and gentlemen, concludes our presentation. There are folders in front of you all with hard copies of the proposal and financial estimates, as requested.

"On behalf of Team Intersect and RBA, I'd like to thank you for this wonderful opportunity and for your time this morning."

Ryan Perry raised his hand in response. "Chris," he said and then looked across the room toward David Ross, "and David," now pausing slightly "and team," he added. "Wonderful work!" He nodded toward Chris and then David and started clapping his hands in applause. The rest of the room joined in.

———

"I really feel like we should break out the champagne, darlin'." Connie was looking at David as they convened in her office on their return.

"No," Chris and David said in unison, and both smiled at their synchronicity.

"Oh, I know ya'll think it's bad luck," said Connie, "but that was a slam dunk, no question."

David's mobile phone beeped with an incoming text message. "It's Ryan. He wants me to call him."

"What are you waitin' for?" said Connie.

David Ross hit his speed dial and held the phone up to his ear. David's side of the conversation went this way:

"Ryan, this is David."

"Thank you."

"Yes, we were pleased with the way it went; glad you were too."

"That's fantastic news, Ryan." David had broken into a grin. "I'll let everyone know. Yes, Chris and Rebecca are with us now."

"Talk soon. Many thanks for calling. Yes, I know we have a lot of details to discuss. I'm sure we can get to an agreement."

David ended the call, and Connie's office filled with cheers. "*Now* the champagne!" said David Ross.

———————

Later in the afternoon, Chris and Rebecca were going through some paperwork in a spare office at RBA when David appeared at the doorway.

"Chris, do you have time for a quick chat?" he asked. Rebecca got up to leave.

"No, don't leave," said David. "Chris, would you join me for a tea or coffee? Let's get out of the office for a quick minute."

"Sure."

In a quiet corner of a café a block or so from his office, David Ross was coming quickly to the point: "I need to come clean with you about the work I've been doing for the government. I want you to know that it is driven by patriotism in the broadest sense . . ."

"I get it," interrupted Chris, raising his hand and trying to spare David from an overelaborate explanation. "I've been there."

"So I understand. When Bobby Messiter at Treasury told me that there was a chance I could be relieved of the responsibility . . ." David Ross looked every one of his seventy-odd years at that moment; he was clearly straining to articulate his feelings.

"It's been an enormous burden for me, what with my friendship with Ryan and my agreement to . . ."—David was searching for a lesser word but couldn't find one—"inform on them."

Chris nodded sympathetically. "I'm rather torn by the request myself," said Chris. "I don't fully understand what's driving it and if there is even a there, there."

Ross looked across his barely touched cup of coffee. "The fact of the matter," he said, "is that the power has rather gone to Ryan's head over the past few years. He's changed a lot."

David was entering full disclosure mode, thought Chris.

"They've been, shall we say, cutting some corners and making some rather questionable calls." David's eyes were averted from Chris as he spoke.

"You mean the NRA?" asked Chris, not really needing an answer to such a rhetorical question but feeling it necessary to punctuate the full-blown confession that was unfolding with clear and unambiguous statements.

"From what I've discovered so far, it appears that the corporate partnership fees may be concealing a multitude of sins," continued David. "You remember when we looked at the NRA business model we discussed, that it was the individual membership fees and the media advertising providing the greater part of their revenues?"

"Yes," replied Chris. "Of course. Our whole proposal is based on growing their individual membership base, as well as their digital advertising dollars."

"There is another revenue source for the Association," David said. "One that doesn't get mentioned very often. The NRA charter doesn't allow for corporate membership, so the firearms manufacturers show their support for the mission by becoming 'corporate partners.'" The minimum donation is $25,000 to become a corporate partner."

David paused to examine Chris's reaction.

Chris wasn't surprised by this revelation, but it sounded like David Ross had more he wanted to get off his chest.

"What I've discovered," David said, "is that the donations from the corporate partners far exceed that recommended amount. What I've also discovered is that the proceeds appear to have disappeared into somewhat of an accounting black hole within the NRA itself. It seems that there now exists a corporate donation slush fund courtesy of the corporate partners—your Remingtons and your Smith & Wessons. The theory we're pursuing is that some or all of this money is being diverted to support extremist groups. And Ryan's reasoning appears to be that in supporting these extremist groups, they are creating a climate of what he calls the 'triple benefit.'"

"Triple benefit?"

"Yes, first the extremist groups themselves are attracting more members and buying more guns for them. Second, the visible rise of extremist groups creates a climate of fear among regular folks, who then start arming themselves for protection from these potential vigilantes. Third, the rise of these groups, which started on the right of the political spectrum, will spread to many groups holding different ideologies. They believe the left is under-armed and wants to catch up. The NRA wants to be an equal opportunity provider. That's what the Treasury guys are chasing."

Chris whistled softly. "OK, I see the problem, but I still don't see why the people I was helping at the State Department are working so closely with the Treasury on what sounds like a domestic problem. I'm not minimizing the issue; it just seems, well, containable. Isn't it?"

David Ross seemed to consider Chris's observation. "I believe that it became a matter of national security after Ryan gave a speech at the United Nations in 2012," he replied. "His address there said that the Second Amendment is freedom's most valuable idea and the rest of the world should be adopting it to prevent tyranny. He's made no secret of the fact that the NRA needs to grow outside the US to prosper. Obviously, the gun manufacturers agree with him wholeheartedly. They believe that the US market is saturated. So, the suspicion is that the NRA may also be acting to support arms sales in other countries."

"And your friends at the US Department of the Treasury ...?" Chris asked, and David grimaced.

Chris continued, "Do they believe that the NRA may be covertly funding foreign organizations that may be in the market for firearms?"

David nodded. "Hence the overlap between the State Department and the Treasury. The Treasury Department oversees domestic terrorism threats. *Your* friends . . ." Touché, thought Chris.

David continued, "Your friends at the State Department step in at the border. Or if not them, it could be a federal law enforcement agency."

"Well," said Chris. "Oh what a tangled web we weave when first we practice to deceive."

The two men regarded each other. One who had taken on the spying mission under duress, the other driven by . . . what? Patriotism? Greed?

Chris broke the silence. "I can see that your relationship with Ryan Perry may have afforded you access to his private schemes and fantasies, but how am I meant to pick that up?"

David Ross took on a new energy, seemingly shedding a decade from his jaded eyes.

"Honestly, Chris, until I met you, I had no idea how it might work. I was just praying that I would be able to hand over this burden. But now that we've worked together and I've seen you in action, I can see why you are so successful and why you attracted the attention of State. You have a way about you. A charisma. People find you compelling. I can see it with Ryan. That reveal of the billboards? It was genius. He will be eating out of your hand. And from a practical point of view—now Intersect and RBA will be responsible for the spend of the combined amount of three separate internal departments. That means a new, larger budget with less internal oversight. The idea is that we—you—will know the amount coming in and where it will be spent. And that will help the Feds get a bead on it."

Chris digested this information quickly. If David was right, the CEO of the NRA was planning to reduce overhead and oversight at his own headquarters in order to have more money and more freedom to spend it where he wanted. That in itself wasn't a crime by any stretch of the imagination. Bringing in Intersect and RBA to manage what had previously been an internal operation would certainly give Perry a freer rein and less interference from his colleagues at NRA. But Chris's task would be to get close enough to the numbers and, more importantly, close enough to Ryan Perry to observe any deceptive practices. That was going to be a challenge. Chris wondered how much of David Ross's excitement wasn't at the opportunity; it was merely being released from his obligations.

"Anyway," David interrupted Chris's train of thought, "the other important fact for you to know is that Connie has no clue about my Treasury connection or the role I've been playing," And then added lamely, "Small though it's been."

"Are you sure?" asked Chris. He found this to be extremely unlikely.

"Yes. This started before we met. After my first wife died, I rather went off the rails. Cliché though that sounds, it happens to be true. You don't need to know the details, but I foolishly agreed to take some foreign money for a couple of lobbying assignments and failed to declare the projects and the fees—which happened to be paid in cash. It wasn't a great situation, and this has been my penance." David was struggling through this admission, his voice low, almost to a murmur and his body language submissive.

Chris not only wondered whether to believe David Ross; he wondered about David's belief in Connie's ignorance. Connie didn't strike him as someone who would be in the dark about any aspect of the business, or come to that, of her husband's secrets. Although it appeared to be true that the NRA account had been

David's personal fiefdom for decades and before Connie had entered and transformed the business.

For now, he'd have to take all of this at face value. There was the added complication that the new entity, about to be hired by the NRA, was a three-way partnership in any case, so Chris would be juggling RBA and Universal as well as staffing up his own New York and DC entity.

There was no official Intersect/RBA yet, only a draft agreement to form a joint venture if they won the business. Plus, they didn't have the NRA's financial terms yet.

That last part did not take long.

Back in the RBA offices and toward the end of the day, Chris and Rebecca were wrapping up when an email arrived addressed to Chris, David and Connie from Ryan Perry.

Chris was still reading through the draft attachment as Connie and David arrived at the doorway of the spare office.

"We need to talk," said Connie. "Let's go to my office."

Perched uncomfortably on the leather sofa, Chris peered through the thicket of silver photograph frames toward the angular figure of Connie at her desk.

"So, he wants to be CEO of the new entity with an annual salary of $250,000 plus benefits TBD," said Chris, reading from his laptop. "What are the benefits TBD?"

"To be determined," replied Connie, her reading glasses perched on her nose.

"Yes, I know what TBD means, Connie. I mean do we know what other benefits he might be expecting from us?"

"Well, it's hardly us, is it Chris?" replied Connie archly. "It's his own money—or at least his organization's. I don't expect he wants any extra demands in writin' at this stage. David, why don't you call him privately? Then Chris and I can talk to John Robins; we'll need to bring him into the loop."

"Will do," replied David as he scuttled out of the office.

"Let's call John," said Connie, immediately hitting a speed dial button on the big, old-fashioned desk phone in front of her.

The voice of John Robins squawked tinnily from the apparatus:

"Well, congratulations again, Connie. That's a big win."

"I have Chris Crossley with me, John."

"Oh, hi Chris," the disembodied voice continued without a pause. "I hear you knocked it out of the park."

"It was a team effort," replied Chris.

"Good, good. What are the next steps."

"That's why we're callin' you, John. It seems from Ryan Perry's first response that he wants to be installed as CEO of the new marketin' agency entity."

"If his bylaws allow for it, that's a powerful play." John Robins sounded impressed. "What is he asking for?"

"250 K," Connie replied, "plus other benefits. David's just gone off to call him to find out what's in the plus."

"Nothing we can't handle, I'm sure. We'll just load up our fees to cover his role, which he'll expect. Keep me posted, and let me know what you need from us. Once we have their formal offer, we can put our own structure and paperwork together. That's a big win, guys. Well done again!"

The line went dead. Chris surmised that Connie had already let Robins know about the successful outcome of the pitch, information he decided to tuck away, like a bookie at the racetrack

Connie shifted in her seat and continued talking toward Chris as if Robins were still on the phone. "We should get our new agency structure and reportin' lines in place once we have their written confirmation and a firm budget to work with. Is that what you were talkin' to David about earlier?"

Chris murmured a noise of assent and rose from the couch.

"I need to get back to New York," he said, "and I'm heading to London at the end of the week. Let's try and get all the basics agreed before then. I assume you're good with Rebecca being the day-to-day account manager on the business? Let's do a Zoom tomorrow, and we can go over the details and accommodate whatever else Mr. Perry wants to include."

"What's a Zoom?" asked Connie.

Chris gazed vacantly from the back of the cab into the stationary traffic on George Washington Memorial Parkway as he was digesting the events of the day. The last time he'd won a substantial piece of business in this city he'd been euphoric and had ended the memorable spring night celebrating with Emily. Now that memory was carrying a severely tarnished edge. Tonight he was leaving the scene of an even greater triumph with an even emptier feeling, if that was possible. Today he had acquired new business partners in Ross Butterworth Associates and Universal Holdings, together with a new client, the National Rifle Association. He couldn't share the triumph with his London team because of their embedded antipathy toward guns. In his heart, he knew that Connie Butterworth—she of the frighteningly dead eyes and manifest ignorance of Zoom—was a betrayal waiting to happen. And David Ross, whose palpable weaknesses hung like decorative badges from his sports coat, looked like a man who'd been reprieved from the gallows as he shook Chris's hand on the sidewalk of 17th Street NW minutes earlier.

Chris gazed out of the car window at the receding needle of the Washington Monument with a feeling of apprehension in the pit of his stomach.

CHAPTER

FIFTEEN

The next morning didn't improve his outlook. Chris awoke feeling increasingly uneasy about being sucked into the politics of the gun lobby and the NRA's various tentacles into the interest groups and commercial entities involved with the arms industry in the States. He knew how to tackle the challenges of presenting the case for guns, tourism and any other commercial enterprise you could care to mention—advertising was the platform for persuasion, and the art of persuasion was the art of advertising. He was great at it. But something so simple was becoming complicated and, well, tainted.

"Be careful what you wish for" he remembered his mother telling him when he had been vying for class president in high school, and while the outcome of that particular victory hadn't been horrible, the recurrence of the memory had served as a reminder.

In Chris's mind's retrospectively rewritten engagement with the State Department in London for the Brexit episode, he remembered it as less of an exercise in espionage, and more like civic public duty. He was aware of his tendency to look back through rose-colored glasses, and as he considered the next steps in New York, he now remembered the Leave campaign politicians and bureaucrats to have been an unlikable bunch of righteous-minded closet bigots.

Chris did, however, remember vividly that he had not been aware until after the vote, that some of the "facts" that his agency had used as hard-hitting truths in the final weeks of the campaign had been fabricated by Boris Johnson and his cronies behind the scenes. The briefly famous battle bus with its vivid message of "We send the EU 350 million a week. Let's fund our NHS instead" had been subsequently discredited by the media as completely untrue. To Chris's surprise, Boris Johnson had now become Britain's Foreign Secretary and someone whom many were tipping as a future Prime Minister of Britain. The only good news for Chris was that Intersect appeared not to have suffered any reputational damage from the post-Brexit fallout. The country was keen to move on from its fateful decision, even though the practicalities of withdrawing from the EU were proving to be extremely difficult. Now no one either remembered or cared which marketing agency had helped the country make its fateful choice.

And so, here he was, on the other side of the Atlantic, taking on an even more unlikable client with an equally divisive message. With an added expectation from a covert section of the US government that he was going to be their inside source. And not to mention jumping into bed with business partners whom he didn't know and couldn't necessarily trust. All these thoughts were stampeding through Chris's head as he sat at his desk.

And seemingly to rub it in, his phone vibrated with a text message from Dai Davies in London: "We need 2 talk. Team not ecstatic abt ur win. Sry."

Chris had known that there would be pushback from his folks in the UK about the NRA win, and he was mentally prepared to strongly defend his position. After all, Intersect was *his* agency, and he was its chief executive. He needed to remind the executive team that they all had a stake in the financial success of the agency. Chris had been generous with stock options in the privately owned business, and he had used the lure of granting "a piece of the action" to his senior hires, most of whom he had recruited from competitor agencies over the past few years. The marketing agency world had become dominated by holding companies like Universal, and to compete with these corporately held behemoths, he'd positioned Intersect as a place to work where your opinion counted and where, as a senior executive, you would have the freedom to express your views and creativity, as well as having a financial stake in the future of the business, albeit a relatively minor one. He'd built the agency over the past ten years under his stated internal mantra: "Advertising is a team sport," and in good conscience, he could hardly start reneging on the premise that had been the foundation of Intersect's collaborative success.

Chris swung himself around on his chair to survey the expanding Manhattan office and gazed out at the busy bullpen-like atmosphere of the floor beyond his glass box of an office. Rebecca Taylor was beginning to remind him of a female version of his younger self. Chris had withstood derisive comments at Oxford and in the early stages of his career as a "self-serving pretty boy," but he had always felt that his looks and his sporting talent were a potential passport to more substantial and lasting achievements. "Let people judge the surface," he'd always told himself, "and let them underestimate my ambition."

Rebecca appeared to be treading a similar path, he thought. Her Victoria's Secret model looks attracted attention that her steely determination and organizational smarts allowed her to leverage. In the few hours since the NRA win, she had taken charge of the need to finalize the Statement of Work with the client, liaise with RBA and Universal as to their roles and responsibilities and work with Chris's relatively new hire, the office COO, George Wright, in lining up their immediate hiring needs.

Chris did need to get back to Dai Davies, however. As well as an unhappy senior team across the pond to deal with, Intersect North America LLC, a wholly owned subsidiary of Intersect Ltd in London, was burning through cash like there was no tomorrow. Chris knew that setting up in the US would be expensive, but the prerogative to provide the resources for the new win in terms of personnel and office space was going to be stretching them thin. The fact that they were going to be in a three-way joint venture had the upside of sharing some of that cost, but of course it also meant sharing the revenue three ways. Currently they were still trying to establish the fee base with the NRA as well as squaring those incoming fees with Ryan Perry's demands, which, at the moment, were being communicated to them piecemeal by David Ross, each one being preceded by a nervous cough of embarrassment.

"Ryan would like to know if we have access to a beachside vacation property for him and his family for four weeks of every year," David had announced on the conference call between him, Chris, Connie and John Robins earlier that morning.

"Oh, and he'd like a clothing allowance of $20,000 a year."

Only John Robins had seemed unphased by these requests.

"Ask him if the south of France might suit," said Robins. "We inherited an eight-bedroom villa in Cap d'Antibes with the Ogilvy acquisition," he went on. "We use it to entertain clients. The wine cellar needs to be seen to be believed."

Chris had not quite picked up the location of the villa because of John Robins's mangling of the pronunciation, which had come out as "Cape Daynteebs," but once he had registered that they would be offering up one of the most exclusive addresses on the French Riviera, he realized that Intersect would now be operating in a different league, a fact that he needed to stress to his squeamish UK employees.

He had been right to remind himself of the cultural gap, Chris thought to himself as his conference call with the London team had unfolded later that same morning. Emily had been particularly vocal.

"Chris, I don't think you understand how strongly everyone feels that we shouldn't be taking on this client," she said, her earnest features filling his computer screen.

"I'm definitely getting over her," Chris thought to himself as his voice responded on a different tack: "And at the risk of repeating myself, Emily, the UK is not the US. Here gun ownership is not only an accepted part of life, but also enshrined in our Constitution. I understand it plays differently there, and as I say, we have a degree of insulation because we are partnering with other agencies. Again, not to beat a dead horse, but the profile, our connection to Universal and not to mention the fees themselves mean that Intersect is a big winner in this. That's currently not an echo I'm hearing from my senior team."

"What about what's happening in Charlottesville right now?" Baz Bushell said, as his face appeared on the computer grid of the video conference call.

"The National Rifle Association is not supporting a march by white supremacists, as far as I'm aware." Chris's voice rose a notch.

"Yeah, but your fucking President is."

"I have no idea what you're talking about, Baz." Chris was losing his patience.

"Your boy Trump said, quote, there are very fine people on both sides."

"He's not my boy, Baz. And I'm not sure what this has to do with us winning the NRA account."

Then Chris added with heavy sarcasm, "Thank you all for your sincere congratulations." He ended the video conference, saying, "I'll be back in the office on Monday where I look forward to hearing how we're doing in our *current* number one market."

Almost immediately, his mobile phone lit up with a call from Dai Davies.

"They're all a bit pissed off, if you can't tell," chuckled Dai's in his strong Welsh accent. "It'll pass soon enough; don't worry about it. But we do need to talk about cashflow. You're spending money like a drunken sailor over there."

"Give me a break, Dai." Chris was exasperated by the video call but relieved to hear the good-natured tones of his Chief Financial Officer.

"Did you get that line of credit with the bank?" asked Chris.

"Yeah, it's all sorted. Let me know when you have the fee forecast for the NRA, and I can plug it in and send it over to them."

"Oh, so *you* don't think I've made a pact with the devil?" asked Chris, relaxing slightly.

"Oh, don't get me wrong," said Dai. "They are definitely not my favorite new client, but I presume they have plenty of money, and that's all I'm focused on just now."

"And what's all this stuff about Trump?" asked Chris, "I wish I'd never got us into politics with the Leave campaign; now everyone in the agency is an expert on politics."

"Chris, I don't think anyone can believe that your countrymen voted in this clown."

Chris was silent. Certainly, the first eight months of "45" had been a stark contrast to the urbane and articulate Obama, who, despite whatever criticisms had been leveled at him domestically, had changed the perception of the USA for much of the rest of the world. Over the summer months, commuting between New York and DC, Chris had realized that his fellow Americans underestimated how closely the populations of foreign countries followed events in his homeland. The world had looked on astounded after Trump won the vote over Hillary Clinton. From the first moment of the dark opening address, followed by the farcical press conference where Trump claimed that he had bigger crowds than Obama, the world's media and their listening, viewing and reading audience had looked on open-mouthed.

"Anyway," continued Dai, "that really wasn't why I wanted to talk to you. The lawyers came back on that JV agreement, and they have some concerns."

"I saw their note, Dai. I think it's fine, honestly."

"I just want you to understand that the 'bringing the partnership into disrepute' clause not only initiates the potential dissolution of the joint venture with the NRA, but also triggers Universal's option to acquire Intersect." Dai was talking very slowly and deliberately.

"Correction," interrupted Chris. "It allows them to open *negotiations* to acquire Intersect. We can always say no."

"Our legal eagles just don't like it," replied Dai. "They pointed out that Universal has battalions of lawyers, and they're worried it's pretty loosely worded, which is a big red flag in their world."

"OK, I got it," said Chris, "but we're already past our deadline on the new agency structure. I talked to John Robins about the acquisition clause. He wants to be first in line. We're a juicy target for them as we're a hot shop that would help their share price. Don't worry about it, Dai. We won't sell the business until we're ready."

"OK, I'll let them know to send over our signed copy," said Dai.

"Dai, I appreciate your concerns. Thank you."

"No worries, boyo. See you next week."

"Dai?'

"Yes, Chris."

"Put an extra fifteen grand in the exec team's paychecks next month, including yours please. That might shut them up for a while."

"Will do. Cheers, Chris."

The car was out of control and skidding across the country road. Chris was wrestling with the steering wheel, and his brother, Charlie, was in the passenger seat screaming at him: "Look out! Look out!" But the car refused to respond; the wheels had locked, and they were hurtling toward the ditch and the trees beyond. Chris started shouting in helpless fear at the impending catastrophe . . .

"Sir, sir . . . ?" The flight attendant was shaking Chris's shoulder as he lay in his coffin-shaped space in the business class section of flight BA 174 to London. "Are you OK, sir? You seemed to be having a bad dream." She smiled sympathetically at him but was clearly concerned.

Chris had come awake with an abrupt start as he had felt the hand on his shoulder, which he had first imagined was a police officer, as part of the dream, and then quickly realized was in the present. He was bathed in sweat and momentarily disoriented.

"Sorry."

"No problem, Mr. Crossley. Just wanted to make sure you were alright; can I get you anything?"

"No, I'm fine thank you."

Chris wasn't fine. He'd been working nonstop and living in a hotel for the last couple of months. He was looking forward to getting back to his flat in Battersea and playing some golf. He needed to develop a more fulfilling personal life, get more exercise, drink less, worry less about work, take a vacation. God, the list was endless. And now the dreams had restarted. He caught the reflection of his handsome but maybe slightly haggard face in the dormant flat screen of the inflight TV system. He pushed the button to move his flatbed into a more seated elevation and gazed absentmindedly at the trim figure of the flight attendant who'd just awakened him. He needed to call Emily Smith he thought to himself.

––––––––––

The executive team meeting on Monday morning was a quieter affair, maybe because of the knowledge among its participants that they would all be £15,000 better off the following month, a message communicated to them the preceding Friday evening via email from Dai Davies.

Emily Upchurch, Lars Petersen, Baz Bushell and Laura James were joined by Dai Davies and Swami Patel. Swami, a second-generation Indian immigrant and Intersect's Chief Digital Officer, oversaw the now largest operation within the agency, encompassing the technology and social media teams. Intersect, like most in the advertising industry, had been transitioning from a world of traditionally trained art directors and copywriters with liberal arts backgrounds to coders, software engineers and digital graphic artists. Chris had moved swiftly a couple of years previously to fanatically embrace all elements of digital technology. The Leave campaign had successfully used Facebook and other social media groups to push its messages to those mostly younger cohorts who eschewed "traditional" media outlets. It was a pioneering move that had been quickly copied by Intersect's domestic competition. The agency's retail clients relied on Swami's group to target shoppers by email and on competitive websites. And the US Tourism messaging had flourished on Instagram under Intersect's innovative embrace of the growing phenomenon of social media influencers. Swami, whom Chris had recruited from his previous position as head of technology at an online dating company, had brought energy, expertise and a new breed of talent into the advertising business in London that had helped to elevate and then consolidate the company's growing reputation.

It was he whom Chris went to first:

"Swami, how are we doing with our New York hires for NRA?"

There was a collective look of surprise around the room, with the exception of the impassive figure of Dai Davies, who gazed into the middle distance, his fingers steepled in front of his bearded face.

"Very good, Boss," replied Swami brightly. "I've got some great people for you. I sent them to George and Rebecca in the Manhattan office."

"Swami's brother-in-law has a recruitment business in the States," said Chris, addressing the room. "He and Swami are helping us find some talent for the new account."

The executive team absorbed this new information silently. Emily, who had briefly overseen the New York office at its inception, compressed her lips and stifled any sound that might have been tempted to escape from within.

"Now let's go round the room to hear how my incredible, award-winning London team are conquering the world."

Chris looked inquiringly at Emily, who bowed her head toward her laptop, a tendril of her dark brown hair breaking free from behind her ear and moving across her pale, high-cheekboned face. She brusquely tidied her hair away and cleared her throat to deliver her report.

Later that week, Chris, by now well over any residue of jet lag, had received a text message from Randy Gardner to meet at the State Department office on Farm Street.

Happy to be back in London and with a spring in his rejuvenated step, Chris breezed past the brass plaque on the red brick wall outside the building and waited to be buzzed into the entrance hallway. London was glowing with its late summer hues of dark green and light brown. There was dust from the pathways of the parks blowing in the air from the month-long absence of rain. Perspiring tourists teemed around the central London hotspots like iron filings around a magnet.

"Morning, Moneypenny," said Chris cheerfully as he approached the small reception desk.

There was a stifled giggle at the running joke from the receptionist as she motioned Chris toward the door where Randy was waiting.

Before he could go further, Randy held up his hand, saying: "Heads-up before we go through. You're about to meet Bobby Messiter of the Treasury. He's a hard ass."

"Gee, thanks Randy," said Chris. "Great to see you too."

"I mean it. He's a humorless s.o.b. Watch yourself in there."

Not for the first time, Chris was having deep misgivings about the National Rifle Association and all the baggage that appeared to go with it.

Bobby Messiter was as advertised. Medium height, medium build and probably mid-thirties, Chris guessed. He sported a blondish buzz cut below which a pair of alert blue eyes assessed Chris like a human MRI scanner.

"Mr. Crossley. Good to meet you." He had a Midwestern accent to go with his other middling attributes, thought Chris.

Chris extended his hand.

"Have a seat, sir." It was an order, not an invitation, from Bobby Messiter, who was clearly determined to set some ground rules. Randy Gardner melted quietly into the background.

"We thank you for your service in acting as our insider at the National Rifle Association, Mr. Crossley, and we have some rules of engagement to run through as well as some paperwork for you to review."

"It sounds very formal," Chris gave a light laugh, which fell on an empty response from Messiter.

"The US government is concerned about the arming of US-based groups as well as the illegal export of domestically man-ufactured firearms, Mr. Crossley. We would like your help to deter-mine whether industry groups are helping to facilitate this trade. We can offer a variety of ways to support your efforts, including train-ing, and we can offer you a favored partner status when it comes to access to future government contracts for your marketing agency."

Messiter was all business, with none of Randy Gardner's informal, roguish charm. The bare description of the covert role unwrapped the reality of the position Chris now found himself in. He'd viewed the gig with the State Department and Brexit as a patriotic act, but he felt he'd only been giving them privileged and early access to something they would find out about in any case. Recordings of British politicians and bureaucrats spitballing ideas to convince the public to vote to break away from Europe was of a different magnitude to that of accessing information from an established and, some might say, already paranoid organization that may or may not be dealing illegally with paramilitary groups and drug cartels.

"Obviously, I'm happy to help in whatever way I can," began Chris. "I have to tell you that we're still in the process of setting up our agency structure to deal with the NRA, and it could be that I am not the ideal 'insider,' as you put it, going forward. As you know, I'm the CEO of the agency with responsibilities in London and New York, so it may well be that I will not have a hands-on role with this account once we have everything set up."

Messiter paused to look at some handwritten notes on white, postcard-style cards in front of him before looking back at Chris, his blue eyes unblinking:

"We have several years of investment in this investigation, both from the outside and from the inside through the efforts of David Ross. He has assured us that you will have the same level of insight as he had and that you will be dealing directly with the CEO of the NRA, Ryan Perry. "

Chris did not feel the need to respond, as he felt his nerve tightening to the terse formality of Bobby Messiter.

"As I said at the beginning, Mr. Crossley, the US Department of the Treasury appreciates your cooperation with this long-running investigation and will look extremely favorably on any and all help you can give us as a citizen of our country. Now, shall we get into some of the details?"

An hour later, Chris was being escorted through the reception area by Bobby Messiter, not Ryan Gardner, who had left the room during the briefing process, never to return.

Messiter paused at the door and extended his hand to Chris.

"Thank you again, sir, and I look forward to connecting with you when you get back to the States next month."

Chris, who had recovered most of his equilibrium through the laborious briefing of the past hour, shook Bobby Messiter's hand vigorously and deployed his well-crafted charm as best he could muster:

"Great to meet you, Bobby. Looking forward to working with you and your team."

Chris turned to open the heavy black door onto Farm Street as Bobby Messiter replied: "Oh, and sir? Please get up to date with filing your taxes. The US Treasury requires you to be always in good standing."

CHAPTER

SIXTEEN

Standing on the eighteenth tee at Congressional Country Club, Chris pulled the driver from his bag. The weather on this first day of October had been perfect for golf, and he had played beautifully. The accepted norm that you always let your clients win in corporate golf had been abandoned by Chris as soon as he had seen Ryan Perry swing his club on the first hole three hours earlier. The man had a horrible golf swing, so Chris immediately decided to put on his own exhibition and focus on the conversation—giving Ryan Perry the occasional tip as he hacked his way around the famous and, until that point, immaculate fairways of the exclusive club located in the Maryland suburbs.

Congressional had been established as a country club in the 1920s as a place where members of Congress could meet, play and plot. The first five honorary presidents of the club had all been Presidents of the country—Taft, Wilson, Harding, Coolidge and Hoover—and the facilities, so close by to the actual halls of Congress, were second to none. The days of members of the House or Senate also being members of "their" golf club were, however, long gone. A six-figure initiation fee and pricey annual dues had seen to that. Now the club was in the clutches of the corporate, the well heeled and the well connected. Chris was delighted to have been offered the chance to play—he'd watched Britain's favorite young golf professional romp to a first US Open win on this very course a few years previously, and he was enjoying the challenge of this fine test of golf on an early fall day.

Chris was level par as he looked down the sweeping right-to-left fairway that led to the peninsula green of the last hole.

His caddie (a compulsory addition in the world of high-end golf courses) gave him a quick word of advice: "Hit your baby draw down the right side and you should end up with a seven or eight iron in. The pin's on the right today."

For the grizzled caddie, days like this came infrequently—the chance to help a very good player enjoy the first-time experience of a great golf course and to help him make a decent score. As soon as he had seen Chris hit his opening drive, the caddie realized he had a real golfer on his bag, and through the previous seventeen holes he had used his accumulated knowledge and experience to help Chris choose his lines and angles to approach the unfamiliar greens and then guide him on the immaculate and subtle putting surfaces. It wasn't often that he had somebody new to the course standing on the last hole with the chance to finish with an under-par round.

Chris cleared his mind and did what he'd practiced thousands of times in his youth and hit the golf ball in an effortless and aesthetic arc down the right side of the fairway, drawing the ball into the middle of the emerald and close-cropped turf nearly 300 yards away.

"Oh, great shot, Chris!" Ryan Perry had grudgingly and gradually changed his role from client and center of attention of the pair to admirer and supporter of this new acquaintance, supplier and marketing partner.

When Chris had offered him lunch the previous week and Ryan Perry had asked if he played golf, the reply had been, "Yes, but not for a while. I used to be a pretty decent player."

He had obviously picked up the British penchant for self-deprecation, Perry thought to himself as he had watched Chris practice his swing before they set out. Like any weekend golfer, Ryan Perry had quickly realized the gulf in class between the two of them, and after a few holes of his own familiarly inept heaves at the ball, he'd ceased to be concerned about his own score and had, instead, focused on slowing his swing down, hitting the best shot he could muster and copying as much of his partner's accomplished game as he could absorb from being in this close proximity to an excellent player and athlete.

For Chris's part, he'd played golf often enough with average and below average players, and he never minded the extra time spent with a friend or business colleague for whom golf was a difficult game. Because golf always revealed character. Thus, he'd mentally noted Perry's dismissal of his own caddie as someone who was only there to carry the bag and find his ball. He'd noticed the occasional nudge of the ball in the rough with his foot to improve the lie, and, of course—how did these occasional golfers ever think otherwise?—he'd registered Ryan Perry's "creative" counting of his score on each hole, sometimes conveniently forgetting to register a scuffed chip or putt that didn't drop. But overall, Chris loved to experience the reactions of golfing partners who recognized that they were playing with someone who was extremely accomplished at the game and whose attitudes—and the dynamic of that temporary and temporal relationship—then shifted accordingly. Which had happened on this sublime October morning in Bethesda. Ryan Perry had, in the space of a few hours, moved from aggressor, boss and host to—and there really wasn't a better description for it—admirer leaning toward fan.

Chris and Ryan walked down the firm green turf of the eighteenth fairway together, the distant green jutting out into the lurking pond in front of them. The large white slabs of stucco wall crowned with the red tile of the enormous clubhouse behind and perched up on the slope overlooked them.

"If you birdie this hole, you'll have gone round this course under par," said Ryan Perry, incredulously. "I can't believe this is your first time here."

"It's a great privilege," said Chris sincerely. "I've known about the course. I never thought I'd have the opportunity to play it."

"And to play it well and in such good company," he added without losing sincerity.

Ryan Perry peeled off to the right to find his caddie and his own sliced drive.

Chris approached his ball, his own caddie standing respectfully a couple of yards behind.

The caddie said, "One fifty-six. There's plenty of room in front; don't be long." Then he handed Chris a nine iron.

"I was thinking eight," said Chris. "I don't hit it that far."

"Nine," said the caddie firmly and walked away, taking the bag and Chris's opportunity to change his choice of club out of reach.

Chris waited for Ryan Perry to squirt a shot two feet off the ground to around a hundred yards short of the green.

"Shot, Ryan," he called across, again without a trace of irony.

Chris settled over his shot, taking aim at the flag. It crossed his mind to try and give it a bit extra, as he felt it was going to be short, but the words of his high school coach, Mr. Fraser, went through his mind—trust your swing; keep your rhythm.

He hit the ball perfectly with a slight fade taking it toward the right side of the green, the perfect chuck sound of the club making contact with the white golf ball, which climbed steeply into the air, traveling in a graceful arc against the blue, cloudless sky toward the green jutting out into the blue-gray waters of the surrounding pond.

Chris looked up at the ball's trajectory, realizing immediately that the carry down the slope toward the green was right on track for distance and that his caddie, of course, having closely watched and measured every shot of Chris's round so far, had given him the right club. The ball landed eight feet short of the hole, took a short hop forward as if to confirm a complicit pact of mutual understanding between the science of the execution and the art of the imagination that created the shot, and came to rest—leaving an uphill putt of a little less than four feet for a birdie and a round of seventy.

Chris exchanged a satisfied look with his caddie. "Thanks."

"No problem, sir. I knew if you hit it right, you'd be close. Well played."

"You gained me at least half a dozen shots today—I appreciate it."

"Not at all. That's why we're here, sir. A pleasure to watch you play."

Chris strode purposefully toward the green. He realized how few people would understand what he was feeling at this moment: the simple pleasure of being able to play this well; going around a famous and testing course for the first time and relishing the mental challenge every hole presented; developing an immediate rapport with a caddie who had instinctively appreciated his ability and guided him, using his own deep knowledge, to an impressive score.

These were the small things of life, he knew. But they were important to him. Golf had propelled him to prominence in his youth, and it had saved him after the accident by getting him into Oxford. It had provided solace in its dual role as a team sport as well as a pastime that allowed for solitude, self-examination and self-reliance. And like today, it had enabled him to gain the admiration and respect of someone with whom he would ordinarily be at a disadvantage within the business environment. It had also given him insight into the character of Ryan Perry and made him instinctively better prepared for their future dealings together.

Later that evening, reflecting on his round of golf and the congenial lunch afterward in the clubhouse of Congressional Country Club, Chris sifted through the tidbits of conversation that he had gathered during the round and afterward with Ryan Perry.

Perry had kept from discussing the details of the NRA operation but had revealed his ongoing anxiety around the mass shootings that had become commonplace in American life.

"I don't mean to be cynical," he had said—before uttering a sentence Chris could not help but observe that was as deeply cynical as any he had ever heard— "but the occasional mass shooting is good for us. It reminds people of the dangers that are lurking out there and to be prepared. But a constant barrage of them—and if they take place in schools—is an open invitation to more legislation."

The word "legislation" translated into what Perry regarded as gun control, something he and the NRA had vowed to resist at all costs.

Like most public-facing figures who found themselves under a regular spotlight, Perry tended to repeat himself often.

"Don't forget, Chris," he had said, as if divulging a seldom shared secret during their lunch at Congressional, "the only thing that stops a bad guy with a gun is a good guy with a gun." Perry's eyes, deep set in dark trenches of shadow on his hawkish face, had a faraway look in them as he parroted his oft-repeated talking points.

This conversation rattled around Chris's head as he woke to a blizzard of texts and email alerts the next morning.

At 10 pm the previous evening in Las Vegas, a gunman had opened fire on a crowd of concertgoers from a hotel room window. It appeared that the gunman (news reports were conjecturing that there could have been an accomplice) had barricaded himself in a room he had occupied in the Mandalay Bay Hotel, and current estimates were that more than fifty people had been killed and hundreds more wounded.

Chris scanned the news reports and listened to the TV news as he quickly dressed. The news was horrific and the number of casualties scarcely believable. His hotel room was just around the corner from his newly installed office within Ross Butterworth Associates. David Ross had even added Intersect to the nameplate at the entrance to the building on 17th Street NW, and Chris hurried over there to attend the hastily convened and aptly named "war room," which the public affairs industry, in time-honored fashion, convened when their clients were facing a crisis.

"Chris, did you bring coffee?" said Connie in her lazy Texan drawl.

As he entered the conference room, Chris threw a startled look at Connie Butterworth, with her cascade of flowing red locks.

"None of the assistants are here yet," she added by way of explanation.

Before Chris could formulate an answer, Davis Ross jumped in: "Ryan Perry is on the phone—he wants us all conferenced in."

Connie motioned toward the speaker embedded in the middle of the conference table.

"Ryan," David said, "Terrible news. We've been managing the press line and liaising with your folks."

Perry's voice emerged from the center of the table: "David—what angle are they taking?"

"The usual, Ryan. But it sounds like the shooter either had an automatic rifle or had rigged his weapon for automatic fire."

"Bump stock?"

"We're not sure yet; you may hear before us. The news outlets are like bees buzzing around a honey pot; they're still not sure there wasn't a second shooter. If it's the one guy, there's no way he could have fired that many times without an automatic weapon of some type. We don't have a name yet, but our sources are in place to check on a criminal record."

Chris scrawled out a question on a sheet of paper in front of him and pushed it toward David. It read "What's a bump stock??"

David Ross chuckled and said out loud, "Mr. Crossley is asking what a bump stock is."

The reaction wasn't as expected in the conference room at RBA.

"Chris—glad you are there," Perry said with sincerity. "Thank you for your commitment. A bump stock is a device that can be fitted to a semiautomatic rifle to make it fire automatically. While they're not illegal, it *is* illegal to convert a semi into a fully automatic. Somewhat of a gray area and one that we're going to have to respond to. A bad day for everyone today—such a shame after such a good one yesterday."

"Thanks for the explanation, Ryan. Let's talk later in the week." Chris spoke quietly toward the speaker in the middle of the table.

The Ross Butterworths exchanged surprised glances while the short conversation between Chris and Ryan was taking place. This had not been the reaction they had expected from Perry when David Ross had exposed Chris's lack of knowledge. Ryan Perry was ferocious in his demands that everyone involved with the NRA account should have vast and intimate knowledge of all aspects of guns and gun ownership.

"So, Ryan. Usual tactics on this as far as the media is concerned?" David asked.

"Absolutely. We have no comment. Thanks, guys. Keep me posted."

The line went dead, and there was a momentary silence in the room.

"You must have had a good meetin' with Ryan yesterday?" Connie, clearly irked and by now badly in need of a cup of coffee, fixed her dark and beady eyes firmly on Chris.

"Oh, what? Yes. Great, thanks," responded Chris with a manufactured air of innocence. "We played golf."

"At Congressional?"

David nodded, and Connie turned away to pick up her handbag from beside her chair.

"So, is that it, then?" asked Chris as both Connie and David rose to leave the conference room.

"Yes, for now," replied David. "There's going to be a lot of media noise and demands for the NRA to make a statement. We find that a week of total silence helps move everyone past the heat of the moment. It also gives us a chance to frame our position. The shooter may have a criminal record . . . or mental health issues . . . or a political motivation . . ."

"And hopefully all of the above," called Connie over her shoulder as she left the room.

———————

Chris's first instinct, following his prior day's conversation with Ryan Perry, had been how such a potential reverse could be turned into a win for his client. But as the meeting had unfolded, Chris had found himself struggling with the reaction—or lack of it— to the appalling tragedy that had unfolded overnight. By their resigned and practiced actions, Connie and David had clearly "managed" many similar situations previously. While his head told him that his client had nothing to do with it and that the NRA tactic to stay below the radar was sensible, his emotions were tugging him in a different direction. He sat at the conference room table alone. It was still only 7:30 am but approaching lunchtime in London, so he called Dai Davies from his mobile.

"Hey there, have you seen the news?"

"Oh my God, yes," replied Dai Davies, more animated than his lugubrious exterior usually allowed for. "How are you doing? What's going on at RBA and with our client?"

"Literally nothing, Dai. It's as if it never happened. Lock down on comment and conversation."

"Mate, somebody just gunned down hundreds of people at a pop concert—with a machine gun by the sounds of it," Dai said in a voice laced with emotion. "It's unfucking believable! It's carnage, man!"

"Dai, I know. I had to call a Welshman in London to get a human response. It's unreal."

"Chris, if fifty people were killed and hundreds wounded in a fucking war zone, it would be regarded as a massive tragedy. This happened in peacetime. In Las Vegas. At a concert."

"I know."

"It's fucked up."

"I know."

There was a brief silence.

"What's your plan?"

"I don't know. It just happened; I'm still digesting it."

"Chris, I know it's a different situation over there and we don't understand the gun culture thing, but if I put my Intersect hat on, I'm not sure that having a client this involved in mass murder every few months is that great for our reputation in the long term."

"Delicately put, Dai."

"Think about it. You'll have a lot going on in the next few days; let's chat when you're back in New York."

"Will do, Dai. Thanks. How's the rest of the team?"

"Emily's beside herself, as you could have predicted, I'm sure. Haven't heard directly from the others."

Chris disconnected. It was time to head back to New York and see how the NRA account team there was doing. He'd had a message from Bobby Messiter at the Treasury to check in next week, and that situation was slightly troubling too. He was nowhere near having access to information that could be regarded as in any way useful to the government about the National Rifle Association. He wondered if there was anything to actually uncover, and he increasingly felt the setup of the "spying mission" could be a waste of time and potentially dangerous for him in his role both as the nominal head of the joint venture between RBA, Universal and Intersect and as the majority owner of Intersect Agency itself.

Hours later and back at his desk in the Manhattan office, he felt no clearer. The tragic shooting in Las Vegas continued to dominate the news cycle with the casualty count rising during the day toward sixty dead as well as the hundreds of people who had been caught in the hail of automatic rifle fire, most of whom were still being treated in hospitals and trauma centers in the area. There had been a call for more blood to be donated, as local supplies were running low.

———

Chris sat in a meeting with George Wright, the new head of the New York office, and Rebecca Taylor to discuss the Intersect NRA team, their co-relationship with RBA and Universal and the current situation.

"Can we put some ideas and responses together for NRA that are a little more substantial than thoughts and prayers for the victims?" asked George. Wright, a handsome black man in his mid-thirties who had come to Chris's notice via a friend from his previous life as a consultant for PwC.

"They just shut me down," replied Rebecca. "Said that's not how they operate, and that was the end of that."

"What about the RBA folks?" George, like Chris, was having a hard time just accepting the scale of devastation and feeling of powerlessness. He had a family to go home to in New Jersey, and while Chris had separated George's responsibilities from the NRA business as he and Rebecca were the named Intersect executives in the four-way agreement, George had overall responsibility for the direction and profits of the New York office. Chris had structured his agreement in a similar way to the UK executive team—tying in his compensation to the overall performance of the US business. George had been wary of having both his compensation and reputation linked with the NRA joint venture and had been another one (of a growing list, Chris had thought to himself) wary of being yoked to the NRA.

Rebecca replied to George's question, telling him that she had spoken to Connie Butterworth earlier that day at George's request and Connie had firmly turned down any suggestion that they respond to the shooting or prepare ideas for the organization to appear proactive.

"How often do you speak to Connie?" Chris asked Rebecca, bristlingly alert.

Rebecca blushed slightly but answered with a clear voice, looking directly at Chris: "As often as I need to."

Chris flinched slightly at the tone of her reply.

"Is there a problem, Chris?" she asked, her voice carrying a touch of defiance.

"I want to make sure we're not sending mixed messages," said Chris. "It's important that we are all on the same page here at Intersect. It's early days in this joint venture. I understand that you have a previous relationship with RBA, but you are employed by Intersect in this case."

There was an awkward silence, interrupted by George: "Chris, I have a big meeting coming up at Walmart. I'd appreciate some of your time later to run some ideas by you. I'll get something in your calendar."

The interruption allowed them to move on, and the meeting concluded with a collective feeling of unease, while Chris tried to engender the last few minutes with a sense of optimism as he congratulated George on his new project with Walmart and praised Rebecca for her continued good work on the US Tourism account as well as her diligence with the NRA team and client on this dark day for the nation. As George left, Rebecca hovered near the door.

"Was there anything else, Rebecca?" asked Chris.

"Nothing work-related," she answered with a slight blush. "Just that we never did finish that conversation over drinks." She looked at him directly, lips parted and with one hand high on the doorframe, emphasizing her stunning figure.

Chris felt a tightening feeling of desire for a moment and then caught himself as the image of Emily Upchurch entered his head. Dai was right; he needed to "play away from home," as Dai had put it. He'd already compromised and complicated his relationship with Emily; he didn't need to make a similar mistake on this side of the pond.

"We should definitely pick that up another time," said Chris, smiling at Rebecca, "but not tonight. It's been a tough day."

"I'd like that," Rebecca said, smiling back, running her fingers through her long blonde hair and sweeping it back from her face. "Very much."

"Goodnight, Rebecca."

"Goodnight, Mr. Crossley."

CHAPTER

SEVENTEEN

NEW CANAAN—OCTOBER 2017

Chris got off the train from Grand Central and stood momentarily on the northbound platform at Darien to get his bearings. The train was the quickest and easiest option to get to New Canaan; and Darien, a neighboring commuter town, had slightly faster and more frequent service from Manhattan to the Connecticut suburbs. His mother had made it sound like time was of the essence when she had called him at 7:30 that morning, and Chris had taken the first available option, as he was close by Grand Central Station on his walk to the office from his new apartment on 57th Street. He walked everywhere in New York, as he walked in London; and although the gridded street system in Manhattan was less interesting than wandering through the crooked streets of London, he derived the same source of calm and reflection.

His mother had been calm but firm. "Your father has taken a turn for the worse. I suggest you get up here as soon as possible."

He hadn't prolonged the conversation; he'd find out soon enough, he thought to himself. And he hadn't dwelled on the family dramas about to unfold as he'd sat alone on a bench seat in the train car, scrolling through the emails and messages on his phone as the north city suburbs gave way to glimpses of the Long Island Sound and the increasingly leafy snapshots of neat parcels of high-value countryside.

A local taxi took him the back way to New Canaan, past the large homes and occasionally vast mansions of prime real estate set behind low stone walls and dense clusters of evergreen trees designed to prevent overly prying eyes. Not that anyone looking over those squat gray rows of artfully and awkwardly stacked artisan stone walls would be able to see beyond the long driveways and high gates that led from the narrow road that the cab was following to take Chris toward his family's home. The neighborhood reeked of quiet, understated opulence and, its occupants believed, class. Chris had cracked the back window of the cab for ventilation and to escape from the overpowering chemical stink of the pine tree–shaped air freshener dangling from the taxi's front mirror. He savored the warm air, the scent of freshly mown lawns and the overlapping natural sounds and fragrances of his suburban childhood.

The taxi slowed as it approached the Crossley residence. The house was more modest than many that surrounded it. It sat closer to the road, and the driveway leading from the open gate was a short loop that took the car to the front door of the colonial-style home that could date from pretty much anytime over the past 100 years. The tall carriage lamppost that stood to the side of the front steps also had the look of antiquity—the green-gray patina of the metal stand, now reminiscent to Chris of parts of Mayfair and Belgravia in London, could have been an original and converted gas lamp or one recently purchased, stylishly distressed, from Restoration Hardware. This was the artful nature of wealth and privilege—its ability to take on or distance itself from immediate identification by appearing to be one thing and challenging the observer to make a judgment: real or faux, original or expensive replacement.

To the side of the sprawling house was the large, detached garage. Chris glanced toward it as he went up the steps to the front door. The basketball hoop was still there mounted between the two garage doors, its unused net now brown and hanging limply down on one side. There was a new paved pathway parallel to the right side of the building with a ramp for handicap access to what Chris presumed was a new entryway out of sight from where he stood. He pushed on the front door and entered the house. He was almost overwhelmed with a wave of memories and emotions as he moved through the hallway toward the rear of the house and the large kitchen, which faced the backyard. He could hear voices, and he called out, not wishing to physically appear without warning.

"Hello?" Chris heard the catch in his own voice, and he entered the kitchen and breakfast room to see his mother; his sister, Claire; and, in a wheelchair, his younger brother, Charlie. There was a silence and a long-submerged surge of pent-up emotion that felt like a physical wave seeming to cover them all like an incoming tsunami. It presaged a kind of tornado-like vortex that landed with his entrance and overwhelmed them all; the long-lost elder son, the dutiful elder daughter newly arrived from Denver and the wheelchair-bound younger son excitedly bobbing his head.

His mother took one look at the long absent, ruggedly handsome features of her middle child and burst into tears. She moved toward Chris, her arms outstretched and her eyes overflowing as she embraced him. Her shockingly graying hair reached up to just below Chris's chin, and she buried her face into his chest, sobbing.

"Thank you, thank you" was all Chris could make out from his mother's muffled sobs. He looked over her head toward his siblings. Claire was staring at him with a hard look of undimmed hatred, and Charlie's whole upper body was now moving backward and forward in agitation and unarticulated emotion in his chair. Chris noticed a middle-aged woman in the corner of the room near the range whom he identified as a nurse or a caretaker from her dress.

"How's he doing?" said Chris, barely out loud.

"How do you think?" hissed Claire. "You're here."

Chris had been prepared for hostility and wasn't quite sure how to take the last remark. Did his sister mean that his father was terminally ill and therefore that was the only reason to bring Chris there? Or did she mean he's going to be even more ill when he knows that you are downstairs, my accursed brother?

Either way, he knew it wasn't intended as an olive branch— that was for sure.

His mother lifted her head from Chris's chest and said, "You can go up and see him; he's sedated right now."

Chris disentangled himself from his mother and headed up the stairs toward the master bedroom.

He looked from the doorway to see his father. He took in the darkened room, the variety of medicine bottles on the bed- side cabinet, the oxygen tank and mask presently unused by the side of the bed. And there lay the diminished figure of his father beneath the bed sheet, which was pulled up to his chin. His head was propped on a pillow—the still full head of gray hair spread out below, like the loose stuffing in a cushion; his face staring unseeingly upward. The late fall light was filtering through the partly closed curtains forming a speck-filled halo around his father's peaceful but blank features.

"Dad, it's Chris."

The stillborn silence of the room reluctantly moved its mol- ecules to allow Chris's words to hang, then fall around his father's prone body.

Chris moved to his father's bedside, pulling up the chair so he could lean more closely toward the scarcely moving body beneath the sheet.

"It's been a long time. Sorry that you are sick."

Chris felt suspended in time and space. If he had heard his own eight-year-old voice playing with his brother come up from the backyard below and through the faded drapes to join the dancing motes of light, he would not have been surprised at that moment.

An infinite sadness settled over him, and he took his father's hand, which had been hidden but was carelessly and barely covered by the bed sheet. He looked down at the once powerful fingers that had wrapped hugely around a cut-down seven iron as Doug Crossley had demonstrated the orthodox golf grip to his son. That hand was now inert; the back of it, Chris noticed as he picked it up and turned it in his own hand, was dotted with brown liver spots.

The silence hung in the room, heavy as a summer's evening thunderstorm.

"I'm sorry; please forgive me," Chris said quietly to his father's sleeping body. He then said, "I forgive *you*. I thank you. And I love you."

His father lay silent and impassive. Chris continued to hold his hand and bowed his head, his eyes unfocused and his thoughts empty for one brief moment in his life.

Chris came back down to the kitchen to find that his sister had left.

"She's finding it hard," his mother offered as an explanation.

"Where has she gone?" asked Chris.

His mother paused, uncertain whether to tell the truth.

"She's waiting for you to leave before she comes back."

His mother motioned for Chris to sit down at the kitchen table, opposite her. "Let's talk," she said.

Chris looked at his mother and saw the determination on her drawn, tired face. He poured himself a cup of coffee from the pot near the stove and settled onto the chair across from her.

"Are you happy, Chris?"

"I'm doing really well, Mom."

"That's not what I asked, son. Are you happy in your life?"

"Yes, sure. Things are going well. A bit stressful, but that comes with the territory."

"Your father is not going to last long. My greatest wish was that you two would come together and make peace."

"Mine too, Mom. But he was the one who told me to leave, remember?"

A look of long-held pain flashed across his mother's creased face.

"It's hard for a family to recover from what we went through." Chris's mother cast a glance over toward Charlie, who sat in his wheelchair with his head tilted downward toward what looked like an iPad.

"The accident broke us as a family . . . ," she said slowly," . . . but it made your father more determined to succeed at work. It did the same for you too."

Chris started to interrupt, but his mother raised her hand wearily to stop him. "Let me finish; this is long overdue."

"You were eighteen, and you shouldn't have been in a bar. You shouldn't have taken your brother, and you should not have driven a car."

Again, Chris opened his mouth to say something, but his mother carried on: "I know you said you'd only had a couple of beers, and I know the accident wasn't necessarily alcohol-related. But after Charlie came out of the coma and the results were known, your father needed to blame someone, and it wasn't hard for him to find the target. To lose the promise of a young life to such an inexcusable accident . . ."—his mother broke off, looking for words. "Well," she said, "he could never get past it."

There was a silence as tears ran down his mother's face.

"What about you, Mom?" Chris looked searchingly at his mother as the years of pent-up grief and rage played across her crumpled features.

"Don't you think I feel it every day?" he said. Tears were also forming in Chris's eyes. "Don't you think I wish it had never happened? I wake up every day hoping it was a nightmare that I'll one day wake up from. But to be shunned by your own family. Your own father . . ."

They both looked downward toward their own hands that were identically interlocked on the breakfast table before them.

There was a keening noise from the wheelchair that was pointing toward the rear garden of the family home. Chris got up and walked over to Charlie. He put his hand on Charlie's shoulder and ran his fingers through the long curly hair, which was the exact color match to Chris's. His brother leaned back into Chris's touch and gazed into his eyes.

"Don't cry." The words were hard to decipher but clear to Chris. He reached down to hold his brother hands in his own.

"Great to see you, bro. We need to get out onto the golf course one day."

Chris got up and walked toward his mother. "I'm sorry for everything. I always have been. Tell Claire that I miss her too."

Chris walked over to his mother, who had got up from her seat, and he put his arms around her. "I'm not a monster. I made a mistake. A massive one. And I'm sorry for all the misery I caused."

"I'll take your car and leave it at the station. You and Claire can pick it up later. "Goodbye, Mom."

Chris walked over to the rack by the refrigerator and, remembering as if it were both yesterday and a lifetime ago, once again lifted his mother's car keys dangling from the hook and walked toward the front door.

CHAPTER
EIGHTEEN

NEW YORK—NOVEMBER 2017

Connie Butterworth, David Ross and John Robins sat around the small table in the corner of John Robins's office at Universal Holdings. In an almost identical moment as the previous occasion, Connie had sat here overlooking the hubbub of Park Avenue many floors below. A bottle of champagne was propped at an angle in the ice bucket, and half-full glasses of Tattinger sat before each of them.

"Welcome, officially, to the Universal family, David," John Robins held up his glass, tilted it toward David Ross and nodded at him with a half-smile playing across his coarse, recently mustachioed face.

"We're very happy to have RBA fully inside the fold."

"And I'm happy to be here," responded David Ross. "And even happier to have this!" he said, grinning broadly as he brandished the check that John Robins had just ceremoniously signed.

Connie winced inwardly and looked away. Her husband had a knack for turning the most memorable of moments into cringe-inducing occasions. Not that this was an insignificant one for him, she thought to herself. David Ross, well-regarded and well-respected lobbyist and pillar of the DC establishment had been at the wheel of a slowly fading public affairs agency when she had arrived in his life. She had provided oxygen for his limping business, helped him overcome his difficulties both personal and financial, and here he was, with a large payout for the shares of his lifetime's labors to show for it. It had been a good trade though, no question. Connie, the copper-haired and fiercely ambitious daughter of the eternally well-respected Robert Butterworth Jr.—he who put the "worth" into Fort Worth in Connie's endless retelling of it—not only had found a match but had gained access to the incestuous high society of the Washington DC establishment.

And boy, had she made up for lost time, she smiled to herself. The lack of respect she had felt in Dallas, being constantly referred to as "Bobby Butterworth's girl," had been replaced by admiration and respect in the claustrophobic confines of the Inner Beltway club. "You saved that man" she'd been told more than once by her new and bejeweled friends. She'd resuscitated him for sure, as she injected her own money into the many charities, balls and social events and revitalized the newly rechristened Ross Butterworth Associates into its previous role as a major political force in the town.

"It was a good trade," she said quietly and out loud.

Connie caught herself with a start as the two men looked across at her. "It was a good deal," she said, "for all of us. We are happy to be fully inside the tent, John. Cheers!" Connie raised her glass toward John Robins.

"How's it going with Intersect?" Robins asked, never one for too much small talk and bringing the conversation to the business in hand.

"Well, another shooting is an additional cross for us all to bear, I'm afraid." David Ross moved his expression from delight to concern with a flick of a facial switch honed from many years of practice.

He and Connie had been boarding their flight to La Guardia the previous day when another mass shooting made headlines, this one at a church in Texas. A gunman with a semiautomatic rifle had entered the First Baptist Church in Sutherland Springs and opened fire on the congregation. So far twenty-two people had been reported dead, excluding the gunman, who appeared to have shot himself during a high-speed car chase away from the church. News of this latest incident had been broken to a nation still trying to digest the scale of the Las Vegas shooting only a month earlier.

"I'm not sure he has the stomach for it," Connie said abruptly. "Chris Crossley," she added by way of explanation.

John Robins and David Ross looked at her expectantly, waiting for a continuation.

"Honestly, I think he may have spent too long in the UK. I suspect he's a bit of a snowflake. He might not be a great fit for the NRA, especially where we find ourselves now with all these shootin's. What do you think, darlin'?"

Connie looked across the table at David Ross, who hesitated before responding. "Well, Ryan Perry likes him," he replied cautiously, unsure where Connie was going with this.

"You boys and your golf games," Connie said dismissively.

"And he likes Rebecca too."

Connie snorted derisively, "What's not to like? Anyway, she's one of ours."

"What are you saying?" asked John Robins carefully.

Connie paused and looked across, weighing her words: "All I'm saying is that he's obviously a good ad guy—and a good golfer."

She looked across at David and continued, "He undoubtedly helped us win the business, and now we have a co-owned entity with his agency. We mustn't forget that we also now have the whole of NRA's public affairs, lobbyin', PR, advertising, design and media embedded as part of our new operation. We think a $50 million revenue forecast is just scratchin' the surface, don't we, darlin'?"

David Ross and John Robins continued to focus on Connie with close attention.

"Now that Universal fully owns RBA, it owns 60% of the joint venture. So, John, if you were to decide to acquire Intersect's share at some point, I just want you to know that with David's existin' relationship with Ryan, I don't think we'd have any problems pickin' up the slack if Chris Crossley were to leave."

Robins digested Connie's words. Then he said, "That might cost a little more than we'd like to pay, and as you say, we have the majority in any case."

He looked over toward Connie, who was leaning slightly backward in her chair, her long fingers, like the tendrils of an exotic plant, holding the glass of champagne precariously before her, the veins in her chalk-white neck pulsing noticeably.

"What if," she said, her Texan accent becoming more pronounced. "What if you had the opportunity to acquire his whole agency at a discount?"

John Robins unconsciously rubbed his newly acquired mustache with the back of his crooked forefinger like a cartoon villain. "Tell me more," he said.

"I have some ideas we can discuss soon," smirked Connie, setting her now empty glass on the table, her dead black eyes gleaming.

David Ross picked up his check from the same table and slipped it into his inside jacket pocket. He felt sick to his stomach.

CHAPTER

NINETEEN

"By the way, to get to Bentonville, Arkansas, by air, look for Fayetteville on the departure board, first making sure that you have *not* chosen the flight to Fayetteville, North Carolina, by mistake. Alternatively, look out for the three-letter airport code of XNA. Don't ask me what it stands for!".

These had been Chris's instructions from George via email the night before Chris found himself at New York's La Guardia Airport.

George Wright had been a senior figure in PwC's retail practice when Chris lured him over to head up Intersect's New York office. Chris had heard great things about George and had not been disappointed in the few months since he had joined. George had a calm and thoughtful presence and enough experience to let go of the parts of the advertising business he didn't know, get on with doing what they did best, while instilling a discipline and process into the notoriously haphazard world of advertising agency life. At the same time, George had assiduously followed up with his former retail clients to introduce them to this "marketing hot shop" he had joined because of the energy and vision of its founder, Chris Crossley.

Chris had been more than pleasantly surprised when George, within a few weeks of joining Intersect, had revealed that Walmart had entrusted them with a test campaign to promote their new format—medium-sized stores. The chance of a foot in the door at Walmart was most definitely worth an early morning slog out to the city's most annoying airport (although that competition was fierce). Chris sat now in the small regional jet, speeding toward a dot on the map in Northwest Arkansas that was home to the largest retailer in the country and the world's second-largest employer, after the Chinese Army.

The plane began to descend, passing over the endless farmland pockmarked with giant chicken coops that looked like industrial warehouses, and having landed, Chris found himself in a modern airport seemingly in the middle of nowhere. A half hour later, as he surveyed Bentonville's neat and tidy town square with the preserved original five and dime Walmart store from the back of his Uber, Chris marveled at the opportunity that America offered the entrepreneur. It had taken Sam Walton just over one generation to grow from a small presence in rural Arkansas to owning 10,000 stores worldwide with a combined revenue of over half a billion dollars. Now that he was clamoring to be part of that success, Chris felt simultaneously exhilarated and conflicted. The NRA deal, the joint venture with RBA and Universal and the spying mission had been weighing heavily on him. In addition, he had a strong suspicion that RBA had more information about Intersect's operations and clients than it should. He'd spent the previous evening going through emails and messages to see if there was a leak somewhere. He exhaled slowly as the ride swung him past the impressive Crystal Bridges Museum—a monument to American art sequestered deep in the Arkansas countryside.

Today was the chance to do what he did best and have fun doing it. He was eager to throw off his self-imposed shackles for a day.

He walked into the unimposing head office with a spring in his step. There was George in reception, suited and booted and ready to go. The Walmart project retail team was being joined by the company's Chief Marketing Officer for the meeting, an addition that would not normally be granted, but Karen Andrews, the Walmart CMO, had wanted to meet Intersect as a new agency on her roster when she had discovered that Chris Crossley, the worldwide CEO, would be present. The purpose of the meeting was to go over the brief for the test campaign and hear some initial ideas from the agency. It was not a pitch; the project had already been awarded. However, Chris and George had decided to keep the meeting limited to themselves to show their strengths and to present the strategy and the initial creative ideas, leaving the rest of the team behind in New York.

In addition, Chris had cooked up an approach with George's help that might help Intersect more quickly gain a larger foothold within Walmart. Chris didn't want to overplay their hand this early in the relationship, but another Crossley-ism that traveled the floors of the Intersect offices was the aphorism, "Who Dares, Wins," and Chris and George were about to try to put that motto to the test.

"Gentlemen, welcome. They say this room has made more millionaires than anywhere else in America. I'm here to reassure you that you will *not* be joining that group!" The smile that accompanied Karen Andrews's opening remarks set the tone for the meeting. The Walmart CMO had worked long hours, days, weeks and years to ascend to her position. She was a capable, comfortable and highly intelligent presence. She clearly and instantly took to Chris and vice versa—they looked for all the world as if they had known each other for years. Their body language spoke to an instant connection, and both they and the other participants in the meeting were immediately aware of it.

"We're happy to try to disprove that assertion," said Chris, flashing his trademark smile back at her.

George, feeling both uncomfortable at not being in command of the room and at the same time encouraged by the positive opening exchange, pulled his chair up to the table and began to speak: "Once again, many thanks for entrusting us with the test campaign for the new-format stores. We have some initial creative and media ideas to run through with you today. Walmart already dominates the mass market, and we believe you have the opportunity to break into a different demographic as you roll out these mid-size stores into more affluent neighborhoods throughout the country. We believe shoppers will want to save money . . ."

"*Live Better*"—the loudly articulated words had clearly come from Chris Crossley, but he didn't look up from the table, and George continued as if the interruption hadn't happened.

" . . . and shoppers will be intrigued by the arrival of a new store in their neighborhood that has a different look, but a familiar name. Our approach will be to create a local buzz around each opening, while leveraging Walmart's unrivaled reputation to allow shoppers to save money . . ."

"*Live Better!*" Chris again interjected, this time lifting his head and looking around the table.

"Is there something you're trying to tell us, Mr. Crossley?" asked Karen Andrews, a wry smile on her face.

Chris continued to look impassively at his laptop.

"The footprint of these store openings also allows us to tailor our messages regionally," continued George. "We have digital and outdoor messaging to resonate with the specific needs and quirks of the diverse neighborhoods where your store-planning folks have targeted these new store openings. In addition to saving money . . ."

"*Living Better!*" Chris Crossley stood up. The practiced interlocutor now had the attention and intrigue of the room fully focused on his powerful presence and handsome features.

"Your tagline is 'Save Money. Live Better,'" said Chris. "We've noticed a lot—and I mean a lot—of Save Money messages in all your advertising and communications, but hardly any—and by that, I mean virtually *no*—Live Better messages."

"The core of our campaign for the new-format stores," continued George, picking up the thread seamlessly, "will be to encourage people to Live Better by shopping at Walmart."

"Everyone knows Walmart for its low prices," said Chris. "No one expects you to show them how to use those savings with imagination and style."

"And the beauty of this approach," added George, "is that you remain rooted in your core message—Save Money. Live Better."

"It's just that we are going to emphasize the Live Better," added Chris. "Our research will show you that it's a message that resonates much more positively with your shoppers. But the communications need to be smart, direct and no-nonsense. Stand by because we're about to take you through a raft of ideas from your own new Live Better online presence with a celebrity chef—more Rachael Ray than Anthony Bourdain, in case you're wondering—home make-over experts, DIY enthusiasts, all with tie-ins to the audiences of existing TV shows and channels and then onto a major regional influencer campaign that is going to blow you away!"

"Please type the URL 'walmartlivebetter.com' into your browsers and all will be revealed . . ." said George.

Chris turned toward Karen, and the sweep of his eye and energy encompassed her and then the rest of her team around the table.

A moment passed as everyone started to explore the work on their screens.

"I'm going to have to leave you in the capable hands of Pam and the rest of the team," said Karen. "I'm afraid I'm double-booked, but I'm glad I took the time to sit in and meet you both," she said as she nodded first to George and then to Chris.

"And Chris, please call me when you get back to New York. I really think you're onto something with the Live Better messaging. We may be able to divert some spend or ask you to take on another campaign to include this message. Our lead agency is struggling; you guys may be able to show them how to do it."

Chris stood up and inclined his head toward Karen, stretching out his hand to shake hers. She ignored the hand and came forward to him, engulfing him in a tight hug.

"That's how we do it here," she said as she smiled; then she turned and left the room.

"Wow!" said Pam Riskin, the ranking Walmart marketing lead, once the meeting had reset. "I've rarely seen Karen so engaged—you guys are awesome!" she gushed.

"Do you think she meant it about taking on a mainstream campaign?" asked George.

"Absolutely. Ogilvy is really behind the eight ball right now. Even I can see that we need to stop talking about prices every second of the damn day and give our shoppers a more meaningful message."

Chris was quietly ecstatic. The day trip to Bentonville had been the tonic he required. He had escaped the shadow of the NRA and the clutches of both his partners and the Treasury for a brief, blissful moment. He'd made a strong impression on a new client and potentially increased Intersect's share of their budget. And at the expense of one of Universal's top agencies, he suddenly realized.

December in Manhattan was a wonderland of street vendors, the smell of roasting chestnuts, expansive, glittering store windows and ... traffic. Before he headed back over to London, Chris was providing a small festive gathering for the New York office in a private room at the rear of the Gramercy Tavern. It had been a good end to the year, with the US Tourism business garnering industry awards that were putting Intersect on Santa's shopping list for clients looking to take advantage of the buzz.

The staff needed a night out to let off steam, and they were about to get it. The New York personnel numbers were growing, but the core team had been fully stretched; and Rebecca Taylor for one, whose enlarged photograph from the NRA pitch photo shoot now adorned the office wall of her cubicle under the splashy head-line "Smokin' Hottie," was determined to fully enjoy the evening.

Chris was also ready to let his hair down, but now, some might say finally, seemed more conscious of his own position as head of the business and aware of his own weaknesses when it came to partying. He moved purposefully around the room, a glass of seltzer water in hand and engaging every staff member one-on-one.

But from the outset of a boisterous evening, on every occasion when Chris was seen dutifully chatting with a team member about work or their holiday plans, Rebecca appeared and draped herself around him with her phone outstretched and in selfie mode. As the evening progressed and the dancing had started, she'd stuck more closely to Chris, urging him onto the dance-floor, seemingly (to Chris's perception at least) loosening the few buttons that were keeping her outfit together as the drinks flowed. Chris was aware that the rest of the staff could not help but observe this show. George Wright's eyebrows were lifted in his direction several times, and Chris did his best to disentangle himself from the tight clutches of his lead account director; reluctantly he made the decision it was better that he leave early and let the night unfold without him.

As he said his farewells, his coat draped across his shoulders, Rebecca, cocktail in hand and dancing perspiringly on the small, raised floor, raised her hand and waved across at him. "See you at The NoMad," she shouted, sticking her tongue out at him lasciviously and laughing loudly.

The next morning, George and Chris sat together in the meeting room awaiting Rebecca's arrival.

"Are you absolutely certain about this, Chris?" asked George, not for the first time. Are you sure we don't need HR?"

"George, I found the files on her computer and all the emails—with attachments—to Connie. If it wasn't such a poor joke, given the main account she's managing, I'd say we have the smoking gun."

Shortly after nine Rebecca entered the meeting room.

"Sorry I'm late," she said, setting her cup of Starbuck's coffee down. "I'm a tad hung over."

She looked at Chris. "We missed you, Boss," she said. "Oh, and I can't seem to find my computer."

"That's because it's on my desk," said Chris.

"I've been using it to look through all the files you've been sharing with Connie Ross Butterworth."

Rebecca somehow managed to turn a shade paler than her already ghostly appearance.

"It's all legit," she said defiantly. "We're in a joint venture with her."

"Except you and I both know that it isn't," replied Chris.

"Your contract is very clear, and you are in breach. You've also been sharing the US Tourism work and our financials. The result is termination. As a gesture of goodwill, don't ask me why, I'm going to throw in an extra month's salary to help you through the holiday period."

"But . . . ," Rebecca stammered, her face having sped through the Pantone directory to the number that matched crimson.

"Please gather up your personal belongings and leave," Chris said, his face clouded and stern, his ice blue eyes glittering with suppressed anger. "Don't defend the indefensible. You have been sharing confidential information. I am so disappointed in you, Rebecca."

Rebecca Taylor looked with venom at Chris, then George. She swept up her Starbucks cup and headed toward the door, pausing to turn back toward Chris.

"You'll regret this."

CHAPTER
TWENTY

It was Valentine's Day in New York, with the windows of every store and restaurant in the city festooned with artificial red hearts and roses. Chris had rarely felt less romantically inclined.

The past couple of months had featured a whirlwind of disruptive personal and business issues and events, one self-induced as Chris had made the decision, in late December, to move his permanent home to New York from London.

At the Intersect Christmas party in London, he'd been determined to try and get his relationship with Emily Upchurch back on an even keel. He had missed their chemistry at work and the flirty back and forth that had characterized it until he had overstepped the mark in DC after the US Tourism pitch. She had looked breathtaking as she arrived at the Kensington Roof Gardens with various female members of her account team in tow. Her long dark hair, held back in a partial ponytail, allowed her high cheekbones and dark eyes to be seen to survey the room as she arrived. She was wearing a long red dress, daringly slit at the sides and demurely unrevealing at the top, Chris had noted as he approached her, trying to project his usual charm and confidence.

"You look stunning," he had said sincerely.

Emily had looked straight at him. The dark brown eyes that had softly locked with his own in the room at the Four Seasons that year-ago summer morning, her discarded yellow summer dress on the chair by the side of the king-size bed as a backdrop to the by then consummated relationship, were now hard and emotionless.

"Thank you," she had said. "I won't take that as harassment this time."

Chris had initially assumed she had been making a joke. The repartee was reminiscent of their earlier, more carefree relationship; but as he had reflected on it days later, when he was back in New York, he was less sure.

The new apartment, on 57th Street in central Manhattan, was by no means ideal, but it at least had the effect of moving him out of a hotel. He'd been reluctant to give up the flat in Battersea with its soothing view of the Thames, but he reasoned that it had served its immediate purpose, as had London. And when he did need to be in the city in the future, he would have a choice of Soho House or the Oxford & Cambridge Club in which to stay—neither of them bad choices for accommodation or networking. The business in London had the benefit of a strong senior team, with Dai Davies proving himself to be a wise and steady presence. Chris needed to be in New York.

There was no doubt in his mind that the opportunities in the US needed his full attention. The NRA business was turning out to be a high-maintenance account, now with also having to bed in a new account director, following the dismissal of Rebecca Taylor. Ryan Perry's constant demands for additional perks and favors were proving exhausting. The Redskins tickets were still provided under the benign hospitality of David Ross, and Connie kept the NRA CEO on a steady stream of guest invitations to the Kennedy Center and other social calendar "musts" within the gossipy confines of DC. However, their golf game in the early fall at Congressional had ignited a fervor in Ryan Perry to add to his bucket list a collection of golf courses to play around the country. Bay Hill, TPC Sawgrass, Cypress Point, Pebble Beach had all been visited, thanks to Chris being able to pull some favors and the ever-ready private jet account at the NRA making it possible to take them at a moment's notice to the leisure playgrounds of Florida and California. Now Ryan had his sights set on the top private courses in the Northeast as soon as the spring weather arrived.

As Chris had got closer to Perry, he'd made some headway on his secretive task for the US Department of the Treasury. Ryan had revealed the existence of a clandestine committee within the NRA whose job was to liaise with ideological groups both inside the US and, in some cases, overseas. There was an interest he explained to Chris, while they waited for the green to clear at the iconic seventh hole at Pebble Beach, in keeping groups like the Oath Keepers and the Proud Boys informed about the continued fight to defend the Second Amendment and to advise these groups on their own rights as well as point them in the direction of the NRA's corporate sponsors for the purchase of weaponry. Perry saw no conflict here—we'd be equally supportive of Antifa, he claimed.

"Our job is to fight for the right of *all* peoples to bear arms, Chris. Our Founding Fathers were very clear—we support the protection of democracy against overreaching governments everywhere."

In his one meeting with his "spymaster" at the Treasury, as Chris had come to think of him, Chris had passed on this conversation to Bobby Messiter, who had appeared less than impressed.

"There's got to be a paper trail of some sort, Chris," Messiter said. He urged, "Let's find the evidence." Indeed, he had seemed more interested in quizzing Chris on his relationship with

Universal Holdings and with John Robins than with the revelation about the NRA's links with extremist organizations.

"So, are you going to sell your business to them?" Messiter had asked, his facial expression as impassive as his generic buzz-cut features were bland.

Chris, taken aback by the change in topic, had refrained from inquiring why the sudden interest in his share structure and what might have triggered it. In truth, he'd been trying to stay away from both John Robins and Connie Ross Butterworth, his partners in the joint venture with the NRA. He had taken the time since the end of the previous year to take care of his personal circumstances and focus on the continued growth and profitability of Intersect; he had no need of Robins at this stage and no desire to spend time with Connie, whom he suspected had not approved of the firing of Rebecca Taylor.

As he looked out of his sixth-floor apartment window this gray and cold February 14th and considered the day in front of him, he anticipated the meeting with both Connie and John later that morning. Robins had insisted on a face-to-face meeting at Universal instead of the normal monthly conference call.

"There are a couple of other items I'd like to go through with you" was all he had said in his return email. Chris knew Connie was in the city and assumed that she had also been summoned. It was not a meeting he was looking forward to with any sense of relish.

Chris felt hemmed in by the lack of connection with his erstwhile partners and the growing distance he was experiencing from his team in London. He had always sought out the company of talented and attractive people. As he had built his business, he'd been mindful to recruit and surround himself with coworkers (how the Brits hated him using that word) with complementary, rather than duplicative, skills. His own superpowers, if he were making a list with bullet points (also an additional superpower), were his intelligence (his "smarts" in amerispeak); his presentation skills; his judgment and his empathy. "Talk about 'soft' skills," he had once admitted to Emily when their relationship was at its zenith, "—you can tell I used to be a management consultant."

What he hadn't ever admitted to Emily—or anyone else—was that he genuinely felt that it was his position as an outsider that really gave him the insights, the clarity and the edge that set him apart in the advertising business. Being an American in the UK had allowed him to see opportunities unfiltered by local constraints, sensibilities and traditions. The British were obsessed by class and background, and many of their ideas and ambitions were guided by these inbuilt and self-imposed rules and restrictions. His hard-charging attitude and brash approach disguised the self-awareness that he was transgressing a social taboo. Many times, he had won over the squeamish British psyche just by pretending to be unaware of his own crassness. The credibility afforded to him by his evident love of living in London and by his elite local education allowed him a "pass" and to build his company as the outsider who had become the ultimate insider.

Since he'd returned to the US, he'd been away for so long that he saw himself as an outsider here too. He observed what he saw as the predictable and linear thinking of most Americans in business and felt their lack of imagination, self-awareness and irony in conversation. He had been able to navigate his own ideas and positions to take advantage of that, at least thus far. How ironic then, that if his advantages were those of an outsider in both countries, that his reputation in the agency world had been built around him being able to position himself as an insider. His time and degree at Oxford had enabled him to use his education and his contacts to great advantage in London. His nationality had emboldened the State Department to use him as the ultimate insider within the Brexit campaign. And his bona fides through them had set up the win with the folks at US Tourism (who would hardly have hired him to run their business if he'd been a Brit) and now with the NRA.

He had certainly felt like an outsider at his father's funeral in New Canaan in January. He had shuddered from the cold draught standing at the graveside in Lakeview Cemetery—both from the westerly winter winds and from his extended family and their friends. Claire had delivered the eulogy, cleverly editing out the rift that had divided them for the last twenty years of his father's life. People had been polite and brief during the reception back at the house; Charlie had been taken to his ground-floor garage apartment by the caretaker, and Chris, the bearer of the family name and oldest male heir, had been reduced to the role of canape and drinks waiter as visitors had muttered their condolences and asked him politely where he was living these days.

The only outlier from the crowd behavior had been his Aunt Janet. "So, are we greeting the black sheep or the return of the prodigal?" she had asked loudly when she saw him after the church service.

"Fair question," Chris had replied with a faint grin. He'd always got on well with his mother's younger sister. He and Charlie had spent time together at the Cape for quite a few summers with their cousins, staying for long weekends, playing golf and hanging out.

"Your mother needs you," Janet had said, her voice lower and more urgent. "This is going to be hard for her."

Chris had responded by opening up an almost daily text exchange with his mom, keeping her up to date with his move back to New York and helping her navigate many of the questions arising out of the estate and dealing with the day-to-day household minutiae that his father had handled for decades. He'd tentatively offered her the possibility of coming down to New York for dinner and to stay over during his last conversation, but she was reluctant to leave Charlie, who appeared to miss the presence of his father and whose change in behavior was causing her mild concern.

"And besides," she had added, "I don't want to get in the way of your life."

"Chance would be a fine thing," Chris had muttered more to himself than his mother.

Chris sat in his apartment at the breakfast counter and in front of his laptop, going through the monthly report on the NRA business for his upcoming meeting with John Robins and Connie. The business was going to be extremely profitable once the current hiatus on external spending was over. The monthly retainer was substantial and lucrative, but the planned advertising and promotional campaign that was going to deliver bottom-line gold had been shelved while the current spate of mass shootings was dominating the media headlines.

As he got up to leave for the meeting at Universal's office a few blocks away, Chris saw an email marked "URGENT" arrive in his inbox from Dai Davies.

"Emily needs to talk to us both asap. Do you have time? Dai."

"Heading to Universal. Catch you later. Set up a call if needed. Best, Chris."

At the large and splashy reception area in the Park Avenue headquarters of Universal Holdings, Chris was kept waiting.

"Mr. Robins apologizes. He's running a little late." The receptionist was politely firm.

Chris sat down in one of the many soft black leather sofas arranged across the floor in front of a bank of dozens of television screens mounted in a square on the wall up to the triple-height ceiling and stretched across the whole back wall behind reception. The TVs were programmed to display individual commercials, sound muted, from the many agencies around the world that made up the largest advertising holding company in the world. Every few minutes the individual screens went blank and then restarted with the mosaic of screens becoming one giant, hundred-feet-square screen, showing a single, supersized commercial, the sound springing to life with a Sprite commercial in Spanish, a Persil ad in French, a Ford truck traversing the majestic Rocky Mountains across the prairies to the parking lot of a big-box hardware store.

Chris looked across the rows of black sofas for the flame red hair of Connie Butterworth, but she was nowhere to be seen. Perhaps she wasn't coming after all.

"Mr. Crossley, Mr. Robins will see you now." Robins's assistant had come down the private elevator assigned to the executive floor unseen by Chris and was standing next to him, the flickering light of the multi-screens obscuring her features from Chris's view.

As they entered John Robins's office, Chris immediately knew something out of the ordinary was taking place. There was an expectant air of nervous energy in the room. Robins stood up from behind his desk as soon as Chris entered, his short squat frame gesturing toward the small conference table where Connie Ross Butterworth was already perched. With pursed red lips and coiffed waves of brick-colored hair mounted on her telescopic alabaster neck, Connie swiveled toward Chris. The blank eyes of a watchful crow stared at him as he crossed the room.

"This is our general counsel, Brian Collins," Robins said as he stretched his arm out toward a gray-haired, patrician-looking man at the far end of the glass-topped table. Collins had a black folder spread out in front of him with a small stack of documents within.

Chris said nothing. His mind was racing, and his gut was wrenching with alarm. It was a trap of some kind; he could only wait for it to spring.

Robins waited for Chris to seat himself.

"It has come to our attention that you have been engaged by a government department to spy on our shared client, the National Rifle Association," began John Robins.

"We see this not only as a breach of trust between partners, but in contravention of our joint venture agreement to manage this business."

Chris looked from Robins to Connie Butterworth and then to Brian Collins, allowing the cards to be played.

Collins spoke next, clearing his throat first, then looking down at the folder in front of him. "According to the agreement dated the fourteenth of September two thousand and seventeen," he began and then put his finger on the document in front of him to emphasize that he was reading directly, "if any party should cause the partnership formation to come into public disrepute or create conditions to undermine the confidence of the shared client in the public reputation of the joint venture or its ability to deliver the signed statement of work, each agency has the right to terminate this agreement, subject to a majority vote of the shareholders, as determined by . . . et cetera, et cetera." Collins looked up from the document in front of him.

"Given this information, we believe that Ryan Perry would fire us in a heartbeat, as I'm sure you would agree," said John Robins. "Connie and I," he continued, "are in agreement that we should terminate this joint venture, with this information now in our possession."

A silence settled around the table.

Chris's immediate realization was that he'd been lied to by David Ross. Connie had been fully aware of the previous agreement between the Treasury Department and her husband. It was history now, though, and that fact would not alter the position that he now found himself in. And with Universal's acquisition of RBA, the voting bloc was essentially 60:40 against him in any case.

"I guess you'll have to convince Ryan Perry that you can do the job without Intersect." Chris rose, as if to leave the table.

"Not so fast, Chris," said John Robins. "We would like Intersect to remain as a partner in the business. We are prepared to acquire the business as per the terms of our agreement."

"Intersect is not currently for sale," responded Chris quickly and tersely, again moving his chair away from the table.

"You may find that this could be the most opportune time to sell, and you may find our offer more generous than any others that may be out there." Robins looked smugly toward Chris, then Connie, as he folded his stubby arms in front of his chest.

The pale neck swilled toward him:

"Rebecca Taylor contacted me to report sexual harassment," said Connie tightly. "As a leader of this business and as a woman, this is an accusation that I take very seriously."

"You have to be kidding me!" Chris said. "She's a crazy stalker!"

The words were out of Chris's mouth before he had time to consider them, so incensed was he that the pieces of the puzzle were finally coming together. Rebecca's overtly suggestive behavior, her previous internship at RBA and her friendly relationship with both Connie and David, crowned by this accusation, now made sense to him. The handing over of the baton between him and David both with the NRA relationship and the supposedly secret agreement with the Treasury Department was clearly part of the plot too.

"I'm assumin' that you *have* heard of the Me Too movement?" Connie was on the attack now, her nostrils flaring in mock indignation, the neck quivering with the perceived assault on her gender.

"We have also been making some discrete inquiries in London," John Robins said, turning his attention to Chris, his hands folding to form a tent of supercilious superiority in front of his chest. "It seems that a senior female member of your staff may have filed a complaint against you. At this moment this is unconfirmed, but if true, it goes to a pattern of behavior that the advertising industry is fighting to eradicate."

Chris was finding it difficult to breathe as he tried to absorb the speed and ferocity of the ambush. He knew he had to get out of there and clear his head.

"Well, Intersect is still a private company and majority-owned by me. Your accusations are false, and you'll be hearing next from my lawyers." Chris stood up and looked toward Brian Collins, the silver-haired general counsel, then moved his fierce indignant gaze to Robins and finally his eyes rested on Connie Butterworth.

"You are despicable people!" He walked out of the office, his whole core shaken.

As Chris walked the ten blocks back toward his apartment on the sidewalks that had been cleared of snow the previous day and now had dirty gray piles of slush impeding his desire to push past the slow-walking tourists and unhurried workers, he pulled his phone from inside his jacket pocket and hit the speed dial for Dai Davies.

"I'm in the street. I'll be in my apartment in ten minutes. Get the agreement with Universal and RBA in front of you. Just you, not Emily."

———

"I'm not sure we can do anything about the JV." Dai's sonorous Welsh accent emerged from his grave and bearded visage on the

Zoom screen in front of Chris. "We said at the time that the agreement was weighted in their favor. We can't be part of a joint venture business that doesn't want us and has both the shares and the avowed intention to part ways. I think you need to make it as quick, painless and lucrative an exit as possible."

Dai paused and then quickly interjected before Chris had a chance to respond as another thought had clearly just occurred to him: "You're not thinking of trying to get the NRA to come to us on our own, are you?" There was alarm in Dai's voice.

"No, Dai. I hear you. But I don't think you get it. Robins wants the whole of Intersect, not just to ride us out of the NRA piece."

"But you said it when we put this deal together, Chris. You own the majority of the business, and it's not for sale. End of story, surely?"

"It's uglier than that, Dai." The full realization of Universal's nefarious intention was settling on Chris. "Universal needs a hot shop for its share price, and they figure they can pick up Intersect for a song by pressuring me to sell. If I resist, they will come after my reputation, and what do we always say about reputation? It takes many good deeds to make and one bad one to destroy. We can't prosper in this industry if nobody wants to work with us. Look what's happening with Me Too right now. They're going to put me in those cross hairs."

Dai Davies was silent.

"Did Emily ever file that complaint?" Chris's voice was quietly resigned.

"No, she never did. I talked her out of it. She was so pissed off with you, though."

"I know. And justifiably," said Chris. "I've seen a couple of texts from her. What did she want this morning, do you know?"

"I'm not sure," responded Dai. "She was very anxious to talk and wanted us both on the call."

"I'll deal with it."

"What's next?" asked Dai.

"I need to think, Dai. Put the lawyers on alert. One way or another, we need to get the best out of a bad situation."

"Will do."

"And Dai?"

"Yes?"

"I'm sorry."

As soon as Chris terminated the call with his CFO, his mobile pinged with another message from Emily Upchurch: "PLS CALL ME"

Chris sighed to himself; Valentine's Day was turning into a day of reckoning.

"Chris, I want you to know that I never filed a complaint against you." Emily's voice was urgent and charged with emotion.

"I was so angry with you. But after I talked to Dai and decided not to put anything in writing, I told Baz Bushell about it down the pub. I'm sorry."

"I don't fully follow, Em."

"He was in an industry Creative Circle meeting about Me Too, and he told the creative head from Ogilvy about you and me. You know what a gossip he is. I'm truly sorry."

The other shoe dropped for Chris. Ogilvy was owned by Universal, and word had obviously got back to John Robins pretty quickly.

"It is what it is, Em. We should have talked properly after DC. I was a coward and didn't want to complicate your life and our work situation. Looks like I made it infinitely worse."

"I was having a hard time at home with Brian and wanted . . . ," Emily broke off, her voice struggling. "I don't know what I wanted."

There was a silence, and they both started to speak at once.

Chris prevailed. "I'm sorry for the situation, Emily. I truly am."

"Me too." The words were out of Emily's mouth before the irony of what she had said sunk in.

They both laughed loudly in a moment that brought them back together.

"Em?"

"Yes, Chris"

"While I obviously regret my behavior when we got back to work in London, I want you to know that I never had any regrets about the night in DC. Never."

"Me neither, Chris."

"And Emily?"

"Yes, Chris"

"We'll always have the yellow summer dress."

They both giggled like schoolchildren.

As Chris ended the call, his phone pinged with a text message from Dai.

"Lawyers are on it. You need to turn on the news."

The CNN banner was running under the live footage of a helicopter shot of police cars in the driveway and parking lot of a school.

FIFTEEN FEARED DEAD MORE WOUNDED IN FLA SCHOOL SHOOTING

Chris quickly assimilated the known facts in the latest tragedy that was unfolding before him on this day that he knew he would never forget.

A former student at Marjory Stoneman Douglas High School in Parkland, Florida, had opened fire on his fellow students and teachers earlier that afternoon. It was being reported as the deadliest high school shooting ever.

Chris's thoughts, triggered by the events of the day, exploded in anger. "You mean there's a fucking league table for different types of school?" he shouted at the television set.

The grim-faced announcer on CNN continued: "We know that at least six students and two staff members were killed on the first-floor of the building before the shooter moved to the upper classroom floors. The casualties on the upper floors are still being determined while police continue their investigations . . ."

Chris sat down on the edge of his sofa, transfixed by the images on the television set.

"The alleged gunman was apprehended at around 4 pm in the Wyndham Lakes neighborhood of Coral Gables and is now understood to be under arrest at the Broward County jail. Again, this is a breaking news announcement of what's believed to be the deadliest mass shooting at a high school in the US . . ."

Chris was shaking as he hit the mute button on the remote.

"The elementary school champion remains Sandy Hook," his voice took on the mannerism of a sports announcer, although loud and semi-hysterical. "But folks, wait, it looks like we may have a new entrant in the High School category . . . yes, hold on, it's coming through on my earpiece. Marjory Stoneman Douglas school in Parkland, Florida, may be our *new number one* . . ."

Chris's phone rang, showing a London number.

Before answering, he needed to finish . . . "Yes, folks—*in with a bullet!*—we have ourselves a new number one!"

The tears were beginning to well up in him.

"*Yes?*" he shouted into his mobile phone.

"Is this Chris Crossley?" a polite and firm male English voice was asking. "This is Edward Morton from Linklaters in London. Is this a good time?"

Dai had lit a fire under Intersect's law firm—it was after 9 pm in the UK.

"We think we have an angle to countersue Universal Holdings and thought we would run it by you."

Chris paused, ready to engage, as he gazed at the muted TV screen that was showing a montage of high school photos of the known victims of the latest, sickening, home-grown carnage.

"I'm going to be selling the business," he heard himself say.

Chris threw down his phone and followed it, slumping onto his sofa. Was it too early for a drink?

Suddenly he heard a knock on his apartment door. That was strange. All visitors had to come through reception and be rung up to their destinations. It must be the super—what trivial transgression now needed to be added to this day of days?

Chris got up and walked to the front door, not bothering to squint through the peephole. He pulled the door open—to be confronted by a clearly agitated Rebecca Taylor.

"Rebecca? What are you doing here?"

"You have ruined my life." Rebecca's eyes were angry and distant and her long blonde hair was tousled; one hand was pointing accusingly at Chris, and the other was buried in a large purse with a long strap slung over her shoulder.

The hand came out of the purse, and Chris, on this day full of surprises, was shocked to see it holding a pistol, not unlike the one she had used at the photo shoot for the NRA pitch.

The faraway look suddenly focused as Chris instinctively turned away from her, grabbing the door and trying pull it shut between them. The last thing he remembered was the noise of the gun going off and the blinding, overwhelming tsunami of pain in his right shoulder.

CHAPTER
TWENTY-ONE

OCTOBER 2019—MANCHESTER, VERMONT

It had taken Chris a few weeks to frame the front-page article from *Advertising News* that was now hanging in the hallway to the mudroom of his sprawling rental property. The window of the back door looked out onto the back of the bulky Mt. Equinox, close to the small valley town of Manchester, Vermont.

The headline on the page set in the large black frame left no room for doubt:

UNIVERSAL HOLDINGS ACQUIRES
HOT SHOP INTERSECT

The subheading hinted at the more intriguing story:

Founder Chris Crossley Out As Agency Restructures

Six months had passed since Chris had left the hospital and New York City. The bullet had passed through his shoulder blade, causing no permanent damage. The surgeon remarked that his instinct and quick reactions had saved Chris from more serious injury. Rebecca Taylor had apparently fled the building and was contacted, by Universal's lawyers, at her parents' home in Old Greenwich.

Chris's phone had been still live on the sofa, connected to Edward Morton, the London lawyer, who, at the sound of what he thought might be a gunshot ("It sounded like an episode of *CSI*," said Morton later), immediately contacted Dai Davies. While he was still in the hospital, Chris had decided to frame this as an accident of passion, having spoken to Rebecca Taylor and her parents on the phone where all had agreed that she needed help and immediately consented to drop any accusations that Rebecca had leveled at Chris in her discussions with Universal Holdings.

Chris had not changed his mind about selling the business, though. If anything, it had strengthened his conviction that this was now ordained. The hushed-up news of Rebecca's attack had strengthened Chris's hand somewhat, and the flurry of negotiations and exchange of paperwork had been concluded swiftly with a bank transfer and a shipment from London to his mother's home containing the Seeberg 200 jukebox from Chris's Soho Square office.

John Robins had got a good deal and dodged a potentially awkward news item, but Chris hadn't cared. As he had watched the television coverage of the Parkland school shooting in his Manhattan apartment on Valentine's Day with the sound off and his lawyers in London urgently waiting to propose strategies and ruses, the worthlessness of the fight had enveloped Chris like a cloud of sarin gas. He had at that moment concluded not only that the NRA was a morally bankrupt organization, but that all the people surrounding it had proved to be devious and untrustworthy. It was not a fight worth winning.

Not that Chris was unaware of his own shortcomings in arriving at that inflection point. It had been a moment of clarity that had been too long coming.

Ironically it had been David Ogilvy, whose eponymous ad agency now sat within the Death Star (as Chris was privately calling Universal), who had said it best many years previously:

"Political advertising should be stopped. . . . It's totally dishonest." The Brexit campaign had given Chris a taste of the totally unscrupulous nature of those involved and the complete lack of accountability that had accompanied the lies and the half-truths. The quest for success had blinded him from the reasons he first started the business—he liked to help brands and businesses grow. He got his most satisfaction from finding the insights and the ideas that helped good businesses succeed. Most of all he loved creative ideas. Those were the reasons he'd left the management consulting world—to carry on that type of work and have more autonomy, have more fun and make more money. In that order. Oh, and he had been good at it.

He looked out of his kitchen window at the blaze of fall color that had ignited Vermont like magical and benign brushfire in the past few days. The reds, oranges and yellows of the deciduous trees spread down the mountainside and along the ridgeline where this tucked-away home lay hidden like an abandoned bird's nest in a multicolored hedgerow.

He'd called Randy Gardner in the spring to say his farewells and mentioned his need to get out of the city.

A couple of days later, Randy had called him: "If you want to get off the grid for a few months, we have access to a few properties around the country that are, shall we say, needfully remote. We were very grateful for your help, Chris. Your country would be happy to repay a favor if somewhere in the boonies helps you out right now."

So, they had settled on the Northeast, as Chris wanted to be relatively close to his mother, despite his sister's continued resistance to their rapprochement.

Chris hadn't asked the history of the US government's ownership of this comfortable four-bedroom home set in 150 acres of the Taconic Mountains in New England. Aside from the lack of phone coverage and the schlep to the nearest stores, the solitude and the picture-postcard beauty of the summer in Southern Vermont had been ideal for him to rest and reset.

Before he handed over the keys of his company to Universal, he'd done his best to set up his team for continued success. The agency had been doing well, and Dai, Emily and the rest of the executive team in London had been left in place with their generous compensation plans. Emily had been treated especially well. The restructuring that the magazine article had talked about had mainly concerned Baz Bushell receiving an elevation in the group of agencies in which Intersect now sat in London, a gift his ego must have welcomed enormously. Connie seemed to have some overseeing role for much of Chris's former empire. He tried not to imagine her vampiric glee.

In his necessarily bland final email to staff and clients, Chris had thanked everyone for what they had done to make Intersect one of the most admired agencies in the world and left the door open as to what he may do next, signing off with his new Gmail address for anyone that wanted to stay in touch.

In early September, he'd received a message from a former client at US Tourism. The client had heard that Chris was in Vermont. By coincidence, an acquaintance of the client was conducting the search for an advertising agency for Vermont Tourism, and would Chris be interested in an introduction? The interruption came at a good time. Chris had moved over the summer from self-recrimination through self-flagellation to plain-old introspection. He wasn't comfortably wealthy, although that rather depended on your definition, he supposed. He would certainly need to work again at some point. The delayed reading of his father's will had confirmed his suspicion that Doug Crossley would take his lack of forgiveness toward his oldest son to the grave with him. Sure enough, the estate had been left in the care of his mother, then to his sister. A large trust fund for the continued support of his disabled son, Charlie, had been given over to a New Canaan investment company run by a friend of his father from the country club.

Chris wasn't troubled by this revelation. His father had needed to exercise retribution, and Chris perversely welcomed the punishment it provided. After the accident in what seemed like a lifetime ago, he'd run away and created a new and alternative life, escaping the consequences. The arc of the moral universe required that he make a payment.

So, he took the meeting with the Vermont Tourism search committee. The Governor of Vermont had made the determination to take a radical and longer-term view of the systemic problems that underlay the continued decline of the second-smallest state in the Union. The aging and declining population, the dearth of affordable housing, the crumbling infrastructure and the lack of investment could only be reversed if Vermont were to appear "cool" to a population of younger, mobile, tech-savvy and environmentally aware potential settlers. To attract this elusive demographic to Vermont from the relatively nearby population centers of Boston and New York City, the state had a two-stage strategic plan. In the first stage of the plan the state would create a vision of a marketing nirvana combining all the benefits of visiting Vermont; and in the second phase, the state would create incentives and conditions to ensure that these newly converted entrepreneurs and influencers permanently relocate to the Green Mountain State—bringing money, investment and the wide-eyed interest of the rest of the US with them.

It was an ambitious, if somewhat dubious, strategy, Chris had thought. Nevertheless, the challenge was right up his street. After all, in Britain he'd managed to convince a sovereign nation to abandon its allies and neighbors and pull up the drawbridge to their country for no better reasons than xenophobia and self-interest. And with wild and unprecedented success, he'd managed to convince Europeans to visit a country hitherto unconcerned with tourism by implementing the first example of what was now being dubbed "influencer marketing" with his work for US Tourism. If the State of Vermont wanted someone with a worldwide reputation and impeccable credentials to help it implement its unlikely scheme, he was ready to offer his services. Thus Chris Crossley & Associates was about to be reborn.

He'd called up Eric and Shawn, the two NYC creatives that had helped him win the US Tourism account a couple of years earlier. They were thrilled with the prospect of a trip to the countryside, having never previously ventured further north than Hudson, New York, and were doubly excited to discover that they could continue their trip after the presentation for another few hours to visit Montreal, a city apparently on their bucket list.

Chris had taken his usual care to do extensive homework and present some original research as well as working with the boys on the creative solutions and a media campaign that might just work within Vermont Tourism's very limited budget. Once he had won the account, it would be a good way for him to restart a business and build something new with more robust and honorable guardrails in place, he mused.

The day of the presentation proved to be a challenge. Chris had decided against bringing in account management help—he wanted the Vermont Tourism team to know that they would have his undivided attention and not be paying for the infrastructure of a large agency. They would be getting a renowned agency head without the overhead of a bloated organization. He imagined that the image of a scrappy local start-up would be infinitely preferred to a slick Madison Avenue operation. However, he had totally underestimated the amount of detail and organization that he would need to do himself. At Intersect his job over the past few years had been to show up, dispense oozing charisma, lead the team and close the deal. Emily had taken care of all the logistics. From the moment he realized that he hadn't booked hotel rooms for Eric and Shawn the night before; that he didn't have a Mac-compatible projector to show their creative ideas; that he'd failed to let the office in Montpelier know how many people were arriving from Chris Crossley & Associates, another British-learned idiom crept into his crowded brain. Yes, he was definitely in danger of "spoiling the ship for a ha'porth of tar."

Montpelier, Vermont, known mainly through trivia quizzes as being the only state capital in the country without a McDonald's restaurant, felt more like a small village than a town, despite its gold-domed Capitol building; and that morning, the incongruous sight of the besuited Chris Crossley and his two hipster creatives struggling down State Street with their creative boards and projection equipment brought a smile to grizzled Vermonters heading for their morning cups of coffee.

The presentation itself had gone well enough at the beginning. Chris had taken charge of the room and given a compelling vision of the future role of the State of Vermont as a "climate refuge" haven. Far away from the rising seawater levels of the coastline communities, insulated from future shortages by its abundant sources of fresh drinking water and far away from the wildfires, hurricanes and tornadoes that would continue to challenge much of the rest of the country, Vermont was poised for future growth based on its location alone. Its immediate growth issues were economic and social—rural communities with little industry, no population centers of note and an absence of communication infrastructure meant that some other Northern states had advantages that Vermont would need to combat through an aggressive marketing campaign. And by a wonderful confluence of timing and coincidence, Chris Crossley & Associates was available to lead that charge.

Chris had paused at this point and surveyed the room before the big creative reveal. In a moment of almost otherworldly existential perspective, he was floating on the ceiling regarding the audience below of badly dressed middle-aged white men, and he saw himself and his two creatives as creatures from a different planet. "Know your audience" had been a mantra he'd embraced and taught during Intersect's ascendency, and he suddenly and clearly saw the plain-speaking folk gathered around the conference room table of the shabby room in this small rural town and wondered what the hell he was doing.

Chris's hands were gesturing toward the screen with just the right amount of cufflinked white shirt protruding from the gray super-worsted cloth of his immaculately tailored Brioni suit. His voice stopped suddenly, mid-sentence. "Over to you guys," he said.

The two creatives, Eric and Shawn, looked at Chris nonplussed. This was not how they had rehearsed it the previous evening. They scrambled to get their boards out and to walk the assembled audience through the creative approach. Chris was meant to have segued them much more smoothly into their section, but they were pros and took it in their collective stride.

Half an hour later it was question time. The executive with overall responsibility for the Vermont Tourism Office, Bill Orton, cleared his throat to speak: "Well, Chris—and gentlemen," he said, nodding toward Eric and Shawn, "thank you for, um, a very interesting, um, presentation and so on. Any questions from the group?" He looked around at his colleagues. There was no response, and an awkward silence ensued.

"Well, um, I guess I have one question then, about the main campaign idea," said Orton. "While I, um, liked The Green State . . . um, is there another, um, idea at all?"

"As we mentioned," said Chris speaking from a sitting position, "given the research, the geography, the opportunity and the potential audience, we think this is by far the strongest positioning for the campaign. Is there a problem with it?"

Bill Orton hesitated and looked around the table for support.

"Well, um, it's just that we have a beer here called that. Um, Green State."

"Maybe they can help sponsor the campaign," Chris replied, perhaps a little glibly. He continued, this time rising to his feet and speaking, arms outstretched, in his rich baritone to the group of men gathered around the conference table: "As we said, when we took you through the rationale, we fully understood that you are already called the Green Mountain State. The Green State campaign plays off that—and it stakes out a claim for you that's going to be monumentally important for the future—and will be *your* clear differential. You need to *own* the descriptor. The Green State. Make it yours. So many other states are going to be trying to stake that claim. Not only is it already true of Vermont, but you've had the foresight to attach the name to your mountains, and now I'm hearing, you've had the foresight to establish a beer pre-christened with the campaign slogan. I think that's the most awesome news!"

The soliloquy was delivered with Chris's trademark passion and was finished with a dazzling smile.

Bill Orton, like so many others before him in boardrooms and meeting rooms from London to New York and Arlington, Virginia, acquiesced with a slight nod of his head and straightened his papers in front of him. "Um, you'll be hearing from us. Thank you for the presentation."

Chris shook hands with Eric and Shawn in the parking lot next to the Winooski River, which glittered translucently under the autumnal sunshine. "Guys, many thanks. Great to see you. Wonderful job."

Eric and Shawn, one taller one shorter, one clean-shaven and one be-stubbled, respectively, responded with smiles.

"It was fun. Thanks for asking." Eric was searching in his pockets for his car key, something alien to him in Manhattan.

"Do you think the Vermont version of a redneck is a green-neck?" Shawn, the dry, quiet one in the double act, asked.

Chris roared with laughter. "We should have worked that in," he guffawed.

"May not have gone down that well," Eric said as he produced the key to their rental car from his jean jacket pocket with a flourish.

"Bon voyage à Montreal," said Chris. "I'll let you know when I hear anything."

Two days later, Chris was outside on the deck with his laptop on the long bench seat in the crisp fall sunshine when his mobile phone rang. Bill Orton's name appeared on the screen.

"Um, is that Chris Crossley?"

"Yes, Bill?"

"Well, um, I had been going to call you with some good news, but, um, I just had a strange phone call that, um, mebbe you can, um, explain."

"Yes?"

"A woman. Um, I wrote her name down somewhere; um, let me see. Yes, here it is. Um, Connie Ross Butterfield."

"Butterworth." Chris's stomach contracted reflexively.

"Um, yes, that's right. Butterworth. She says she bought your company and that you are, um, prohibited from working in the tourism industry for two years."

"Go on, Bill."

"She said you signed a contract, and her company was the largest in the world and that they would, um, sue you and us if we appointed you."

Chris could see in his mind the mass waves of red hair framing a white pinched face with the dead undersea eyes.

"Bill, I'm sorry you got that call. I don't wish to put you or the State of Vermont in a difficult position. I believe they are wrong, but please let me make a call or two and get back to you this afternoon. Again, I apologize for this situation."

Chris hit his Dai Davies speed dial and was grateful that his former CFO picked up immediately.

Davies was first to speak. "Chris I was about to call you. Cruella just emailed me to get your noncompete agreement sent over to Universal asap."

Ordinarily Chris would have laughed out loud at this new and highly appropriate nickname for Connie, but he was incensed.

"What the fuck, Dai? How did she know I was pitching? It's a tiny piece of business. What the fuck is the matter with these people?"

Chris knew the answers, of course. Just as he knew now that he wouldn't be able to sign the Vermont Tourism account. He'd hoped to keep everything below the radar; and given that Universal had acquired his former agency at such a steal and had much bigger fish to fry, he'd hoped to appeal to John Robins's better side once he had the deal signed. He had underestimated the underlying animosity that sat within the woman whose father had proverbially put the worth into Fort Worth.

Chris's mobile buzzed. It was a text message from Emily Upchurch. They had spoken briefly but warmly before Chris left Manhattan for Vermont in the late spring. She had shared that she thought her marriage was in trouble but was going to do her best to patch it up, for the sake of their child.

"Hope ur ok. Leaving Brian. Looking to get away for a break w Justin. I hear VT is great? ☺ xx"

Chris smiled. He looked at the expanse of lawn that ran down to the rushing and rock-strewn stream bisecting the property. The gold and amber leaves of the ash and maple trees reflected the bright autumn sunshine of the glorious day in the Green State, as he would now forever refer to it. This eventful year's foliage was naturally fading and dropping. New leaves would not emerge until the other side of the long New England winter that lay ahead.

Chris sighed. He felt nothing but hope in his heart.

ACKNOWLEDGMENTS

With many thanks to Jay Heinrichs for his detailed critique, helpful suggestions and continuous encouragement. Thanks also to my first reader—Cindy Marshall—for her astute insights and support. Proofreading and copy-editing services were painlessly provided by Patty Wallenburg and her team. I leaned on a book by Frank Smyth helpfully entitled *The NRA—The Unauthorized History* for background on that particular can of worms.

ABOUT THE AUTHOR

Craig Waller lives in Southern Vermont with his spouse, Cindy Marshall, and six-year-old Labrador, Sunny.